# *Love Is*

# *Fragile*

## By
## DR JESSICA JUDE ZIEGLER &
## JACQUELINE FARRUGIA MASOTTO
## M.A.

# DEDICATION

**For Mama**
**-JJZ**

**For Mom**
**-JFM**

Dedicated to the Memory of our Moms

Ana Virgilia Pierce Guido

Pauline Mizzi Farrugia

# Acknowledgment

Many thanks to our conspirator, Kristen Jackson, who helped lead the charge between the tears. I would also like to acknowledge my dear husband, Dennis James Ziegler, for all his input and advice, you are the love of my life. This goes without saying: Jackie Masotto, I am not sure if this would have been possible without you, you are amazing. Thank you so very much to Mr. Kevin Hackbarth for your incredible creativity with the cover art. I am very grateful to all my friends who in more ways than one contributed and encouraged me to create this love story. To my dear friend Terry Yohn, I never gave up on you, thanks for your contribution. Finally, to our readers I am grateful and hopeful you will enjoy taking this journey with us.

Warm Regards,

Jess

Many long hours, dedication and fun went into writing this book, which was only possible because of the incredible Jessica Ziegler. Thank you for everything. I want to thank my wonderful husband Matthew: your love and support means the world to me. To my beautiful daughters Cassidy and Sienna: thank you for giving my life purpose and happiness. Thank you to my in-laws, close friends, and extended family, as well. Lastly, I am forever grateful to my ever-loving parents for giving me the tools.

Jackie

# 1

## Doctor Sullivan

LOVE IS FRAGILE and there is nothing that can be said or done to change the outcome of this story, but no matter it is a story that needs to be told. Doctor Sullivan, aka Sully, to his friends and neighbors, took a deep breath, but that phrase took over his mind and he could not stop thinking about the fragility of life, love, and how easily it all can be lost. He kept saying to himself: I am not sure how to explain the events that took place, but I really need to tell someone how it all unfolded. He made his way home and stood silently outside his front door. As Sully looked around his wrap-around porch, he tallied the things he had: a good home, a career, stability. He sat on the steps looking at the city as it burned; the smoke was thick, and the smell lingered for miles. Sully was safe from the hot zone, but there he stood, devastated. His legs got weaker and standing was almost impossible because the events of the riots (and more) had finally taken a toll on him. Sully desperately needed to sit and allow his emotions to pour out of his body.

The door cracked open and a small-figured lady walked out and said in a soft voice, "Are you alright? Did you get hurt?"

"No, I am fine. It was a long night and a long couple of days. It is going to take longer to recover from this one." Sully responded as his heavy body collapsed on the steps. She could hear the heartbreak coming from his words as she sat next to him. "This one was bad. Tell me when you are ready. I will be here."

Dr. Sullivan sat silent for a bit simply holding his head with both hands and then took his wife's hand. "Darling," he said," I know you are strong, but this one might hurt." As he took a deep breath, "I am so sorry, I know it will hurt."

Sully began telling his wife what he experienced the days prior. "I was assigned to the ER as many of us had been told to be ready. We knew it was just a matter of time before the peaceful protests became riots. Riots lead to police standoffs and injuries, lots of injuries, on both sides. All medical personnel needed to be vigilant and prepared when the ambulances began dumping bodies. The staff was ready and all the equipment was set. You know I've been through this before in Chicago and Seattle, but many of my colleagues were clueless."

"It was not long before the air shifted and silence was broken with the deafening sounds of sirens. The madness of the streets had awakened when daylight was lost. The darkness seemed to allow the fury to take over and mangled bodies were arriving. In a matter of seconds, all our rooms: waiting rooms, hallways, and the ambulance bay were filled. It was mass casualties which equals triage and adrenaline. I am not sure how many people I took care of and how I got through it all. There was a sea of people, some with minor injuries like OC Pepper spray decontamination, dehydration, minor cuts, and bruises.  Others were seriously injured: a security guard had burns on his hands, and many had broken ribs. I assisted with two stabbings and helped a man who took an awful beating. We finally had a handle on things by closing the ER and diverting patients to other hospitals. I stepped outside to catch my breath. I did not know if it was day or night. The smoke was so thick I could not tell, but I needed to see the sky. I stood outside and tried to find some sense of everything when a truck rushed towards me."

The driver yelled, "Help, help me. She was shot." I ran to the bed of the truck and I saw a woman bleeding from her chest and a man applying pressure.

"What happened?" Doctor Sully asked.

The man identified himself as a Retired Fireman and he said, "I was cutting across the park. I thought I could go for a run. I saw the officer's SUV pull into the park and a woman stepped out. She was looking at the kids playing in the park and then I heard something flying by my ear. We were facing one another. I was not sure what it was but then I saw her fall to the ground. I rushed to her and saw the blood coming from her chest right above her bullet proof vest.  I started applying pressure and yelling for help.  I heard her whisper a few words. A guy in a truck came over and there was no time to waste so I loaded her in the bed of the truck and we rushed to the hospital. When we got to Mercy Hospital, we were diverted here.  Can you help her please?"

"Get a gurney and cross match; we got a Gunshot Wound to the chest," Sully yelled out as he and Fireman pulled off the vest, and cut off the blood soaked shirt. The officer was in and out of consciousness. Sully applied pressure to the wound as they moved her from the truck into the ER then he yelled out "Grab her gear!"

"William, William" the female whispered.

"What is she saying?"

The overhead speaker blurs out, "Trauma team to ER stat. Trauma Team to ER stat."

Doctor Smith,  Head of Trauma, yelled out as he entered the room "What we got?"

A nurse yelled out "GSW to the chest on 30 year old female"

"Ok people, let's control the bleeding. Come on people! Move!! We need to cross match blood. Who is she?" Doctor Smith yelled out.

"We are not sure. She might be a Cop, but with everything happening we are not sure," the nurse replied with hesitation.

Dr. Smith looked with indignation and yelled out, "Are you kidding me? For God's sake this is a crime, Cop or not, she was shot. Find out who she is and where she works. Someone has to be looking for her. I will save her; you get her people here."

The nurse began to protest Smith's orders, "I don't know who to call. She was brought in with only a gun belt on. They dropped off from the back of the pickup. Someone cut off her shirt and the truck took off. I am not sure what you want me to do" the nurse replied.

Smith yelled at the top of his lungs, "I don't care if you call 911 for God's sake. She is a Cop. Now move and find out who she is!"

Out of frustration, the nurse walked to the desk where a young clerk was sitting answering calls. "I can't believe the way he talked to me. Dr. Smith is an ass. He is there barking orders as if I know who that Cop is. I have no idea which agency to call. With the riots everyone came in: the Feds, state, and locals. For all I know she is a security guard who got caught in the crossfire. Look, do me a favor, call the local police department and tell them we need an officer for a GSW. It might be one of theirs, it might not. Either way they will need to respond and sort it out.

"So I should call 911? How do you know she is a Cop?" the clerk asked.

"She might be. She has a duty belt, a gun, and gear. We just don't have a name tag, wallet, badge or shirt. Whoever tried to help her took off with all our clues. Come on man, she has to belong to someone. Call the local PD and have them respond as soon as possible.

"Code blue trauma room #1" was belted through the overhead loudspeaker.

"Get someone here before she dies on us" the nurse yelled as she ran down the hallway.

"Hi, this is the ER at Northwestern. We got a GSW and we suspect it might be a police officer. Do you know of a female police officer who was shot? No, well can you send someone immediately? I don't have her name or badge number. I really don't have any details except she was shot and is not looking good. Look, I don't know which agency she is assigned to. No, I don't know who shot her. All I can tell you is she might die soon so please send a patrol car. Thank you. Again it is urgent. It is not looking good for her," the receptionist stated.

"Start compressions, one, two, three, clear shock to 120. Come on! Stay with us!" Dr. Smith shouted.

"No response" Sullivan checked for a pulse.

"Push Epi and 200 clear," yelled Dr. Smith. The shock was administered and her body raised from the powerful electric shock. "Hold it, we got her back. There is a pulse. Weak, but she is back. Push more blood. Sully, we got a name yet?"

The nurse ran into the room, "Sorry Dr. Smith, we called the local police and they are sending someone. They did not know anything about a GSW."

"Sully, keep her alive. We need to stabilize or she will not make it to surgery. How can no one know who she is? What about her valuables? What does she have on her? Come on people, we need a name. She belongs to someone!" Smith angrily yelled out.

"Take a break Dr. Smith. I will make sure we look through her things. I got her for now. Go get some coffee or take a walk." Dr. Sullivan piped up.

As Dr. Smith walked out, Sully looked at the bag with the discarded items. A set of keys, a blood soaked Saint Michael coin, and a Miranda card, gloves, and a cell phone. "Oh God please let this work." He turned on the phone and immediately hit ICE In Case of Emergency. No one listed. No listings under mom, dad, hubby, friend.

Then he heard her whisper once more, "William, William."

As he scanned down the list of contacts, there it was '**William**' with no last name. Could it be? Can he be the answer? Maybe a boyfriend or husband. Who cares? thought Dr. Sully. If he is her person and he needs to be here. He could tell us who she is and get people here for her. No one should be alone, especially when they are so close to death's door. Dr. Sully examined the number; it was not a typical local phone number, but this was urgent. THIS WAS URGENT!"

The number rang several times and then a strange static-like tone began to echo along with the ring tone. Finally, someone with a strong Middle Eastern accent answered, "Uh, hello."

Sully was a bit taken back, but quickly gathered his thoughts and went on to ask for William after a long pause, "William? Are you William?"

The voice on the other end of the phone said, "No, this is Bill's phone. I am not sure if I can help you, but Bill I mean Master Sgt. William Young is not available."

Sully could not believe that he got so close to helping his patient, but something was better than where he was twenty minutes ago." I need to identify my patient. Can you please tell me how this number is listed on William's cell? I am a doctor in the United States and all I had for my patient was a cell phone and she was calling out for William. I really need your help please; can you contact the Sergeant I really need to speak to him?"

 After a long pause the voice on the phone said, "I am sorry I cannot help you right now. I need to check with the Commanding Officer and get back to you. It will take a couple of hours to get clearance. I hope you understand but that is the best I got right now."

Sully implored, "Sir, Time is not on our side!"

"Doctor, my apologies, but I am in Afghanistan. There are enemies all around us." Then the call disconnected.

Sully was waiting for the unkind minutes of the clock which quickly turned into hours. Medical staff kept working and monitoring the police officer, but the odds were simply against them. Sully walked to the reception area hoping for some good news. "Did the police send a car? Did they identify the officer?

The nurse looked annoyed. "A squad car came by. They took some photos and secured her firearm. They said they did not know her, but they were going to run the serial number to see which agency she belonged to. With the riots, multiple agencies responded. I am sorry Dr. Sullivan, we have to wait."

He needed to identify her and now Sully was stuck waiting for news from the Middle East. Sully heard the scratchy clicking of the overhead intercom, "Code Blue ICU Room #1. Code Blue ICU Room #1. Cardiac

Team please respond to ICU Room #1. Code Blue." Sully shook his head and started heading towards the ICU Trauma Room #1. He knew it was the officer, but he really hoped she was still in surgery.

# 2

## *Commander Robert Stevens*

THE OFFICER MADE his way to the Commander's quarters and stood outside gazing at the sky for a minute. He felt the desert heat escaping through the sand pours. The night sky brought waves of fresh air and dust. The stars were shining and he wished he was home. He took a deep breath and knocked on the door. A harsh "enter" echoed through the military command center.

"Sir, it's about Master Sergeant William Young. I am not sure what the right procedure is, you see, I got Young's cellphone and he received a call from stateside. It was a doctor, apparently his girlfriend, fiance, or wife. I think she is a Cop and I think she is injured. The doctor wanted to speak to Bill, I mean Master Sgt. Young. I explained that I needed to clarify the protocol, but Sir, this is an unusual case."

After a long pause, the Commander said, "someone called for the Ghost? Was it an asset? Or are you telling me it's a personal call?"

"Sir, it's personal but I believe it an emergency" he replied.

The commander gazed out the makeshift window as he rambled on, "Master Sgt. Young, William, Bill to some but to me he is the Ghost. Bill worked with Intelligence and we will never win this thing without him. The cost of this mission is immeasurable and yet we push through the sand, the heat, the bodies, the pieces of us that are blown off to keep fighting the good fight. Bill was born for this assignment and he should have led the charge. How long have you been with this unit son? You were not selected to be trained by Bill? Why did you have a family stateside? You can't be married or have kids. Not in this unit." The Commander looked up and realized he had fired off several questions, not allowing the officer to answer any of them. He cleared his throat and said," Son, you are dismissed but I will take Young's cellphone. I will handle all incoming calls. You are dismissed and closed the door behind you."

The commander stared at the cellphone as his memories took him back to a dark cave in the outskirts of Kabul. His mind took him several months back and he could still hear the echoes, "tell me about your girl American "he heard a heavy accented tan male whispering in his direction.  Bill stood stern and stoic saying nothing. They had been captured shortly after their convoy was attacked. Only the two of them had survived and now the terrorists were trying to squeeze information. They were thrown into a well and pulled out at different times to be interrogated or tortured. There was no way to know if they were going to be rescued or if they could escape.

Each night right before they got pulled out of the well William would talk about his ranch. He would tell stories about his home in Wyoming. As he recalled his valley, the sky, and the clear streams, the hours would slip away. Bill would say to hold on to those images to survive the torture that was coming. We could not break and give them anything! I held on to his stories and pictured everything he talked about no matter what was happening at the moment.

"Tell me about your girl American" the male with an accented voice demanded. Bill and I stood still and refused to engage. "American men are weak and foolish. They love all women and fornicate like animals. They are never satisfied with one woman. Tell me American about your great love." We stood still and waited for him until he got tired or ran out of smokes.

The well was dark and dusty. The animals would linger close to the opening and their smell would hang around all day. William would laugh and start telling about his adventures at his ranch. He started naming the animals after famous people like the donkey was Jay Leno, the sheep was Rosie O'Donnell, and the dog was Chris Rock. Just as we tried to relax they would pull us out for another long night.

As they dropped the rope, Bill would say: "Here's Johnny! Okay Rob, get your mind straight it's going to be a long night." That night we took a hard beating. They focused on our weaknesses.  Since my leg was smashed up from the convoy attack they hit my leg until I fainted from the pain. Bill got it hard as well; when I came to, I saw that the bottom of his feet were swollen and bleeding.

"What the hell Bill? Why don't you escape? I know you can scale out of this God Damn hole. Why are you here?" He never answered me. William just tried to clean his wounds and elevated his legs.

A few days later we were pulled again and the man said, "Ok American tell me about your girl. Who is waiting for you back home? Tell me about your girl American. Is she beautiful? Is she lonely? I know she cheats on you. Tell me American, who is your girl? Who do you love?" William said nothing and stood perfectly still. The Arab would just pace back and forth until he got tired and we were thrown back into that hole. I began to wonder how we were going to survive another day.

I looked at William and he was gazing at the stars. "Dude where did you go?" It took him a minute as if his soul was reentering his body, and he smiled. "Come on Bill what was that?"

 Bill laughed and said, "Rob I'm sorry. Once in a while I need to visit home." Bill then told me about his bloodline and how he still had family living inside an Indian Reservation. I thought he was full of shit. I mean how does this blue-eyed salt and pepper hair, 6 foot 3 man want me to believe he was a Native American? I began to laugh and laugh, he was so full of crap. But really he wasn't kidding. Bill explained his grandfather was half Cherokee and half Irish. Once his family immigrated to the United States, they settled near the Colorado Region. His Granddad grew up on the Rez, what they called the Reservation. His dad did not want to stay; he decided the Army was his ticket out. Bill did not talk much about his family except when he referred to them on the ranch. He lit up talking about them and their work. I did remain curious about Bill's ability to transport himself to other places. It was Bill's way to stay alive and I needed him alive to keep me alive.

The nights became colder and we had been trapped for almost four weeks. As the sand blew over the opening from our man-made grave, Bill would stare at the stars. He would try to keep up with his stories so I would stay alive. The pain in my leg was excruciating and I was more of a liability than help. I kept telling Bill to scale the wall and run. He simply would start on another story. One night I got a bad fever, and I knew my leg was infected. If I did not get rescued soon, Bill would be left with just a cadaver. The chills were all over. I was dying and worst of all, I was ready to go when I heard Bill say, "Listen Man if you hang on another day I will tell you about my girl." He then threw his blanket over me and gave me his food and water. For the next few hours he would tease me about it. He would say, "Stay alive and you will hear about the love of my life." If I fell asleep I would wake up to, "You missed my brown-eyed girl." I am not sure if it was the extra food and water or his pokes with his girl, but I survived that night.

The next day as the sunshine was peeking into our well, we began to hear the scuffling of soldiers. I thought I was hallucinating as I saw a Blackhawk helicopter over our heads. Two paratroopers were repelling down ropes and into the mouth of the well.

"Master Sergeant William aka 'The Ghost' Young, and Lieutenant Commander Robert Stevens I presume. Sorry it took so long to locate you. Your GPS System was disabled, but we tracked you down with the secondary device once it was above ground."

I looked at Bill and he smiled at me. It seems every time we were pulled out he dropped the tracking chip in another location which put out a signal. It took a bit but one of the signals was strong enough to get through to base. Now we were heading to Germany to get put back together and I had no way to repay him for my life. However, Bill was not off the hook. I needed to know about his brown-eyed girl.

# 3

## *Germany*

THE LANDING IN Germany was pretty rough. We were ripped out of the Huey with excipient speed. The medics were great and I had no complaints but I was not naïve. I knew recovery was going to be long and hard. I needed to know Bill was alright. We were moving so fast I could not find him. I began to panic as the medical staff were checking on my leg and taking my vitals. My heart rate must have been off the chart when I heard a strong female's voice yell out.

"Lieutenant Stevens, if you don't do your part I am going to drop you off in the ocean."

"Ma'am, where is Master Sergeant Young?"

"The Ghost?" she replied, "He is unbelievably stable. We got him and he is sharing Intel while we take care of his medical needs. So, relax, your buddy is good." That was a great relief but Bill needed to come clean and I wanted to know more about his girl.

Rob finally settled into his room and he kept wondering how Bill was doing. Rob looked at his injuries and it finally hit him how much damage his body had sustained. The drugs he received inbound were finally kicking in. He began to drift off to sleep but his mind kept taking him back to the well. Rob's body began to convulse from the panic attacks and post-traumatic stress. He called out, "Damn it Bill, go!"

As his subconscious struggled to make out the images of sand, dust, gunfire, and their Hummer flipping over, Rob could hear Bill calling for him. Rob started reaching for Bill and he started screaming. This is when he heard:

"Dude, I am here. Come on, wake up! Come on Rob! You are safe and we are home!"

Rob snapped out of it and opened his eyes to see his friend.

"Man, I thought we were back in that snake pit. How long was I out?"

Bill took a deep breath, "Rob you had at least three surgeries to repair your leg and clean up the infection. I don't know if this might be hard to hear, but you have been out for almost seven days. We called your folks and told them you were safe. Your Mom said she would fly here if you needed her. I told her to sit tight and be ready to meet you in Hawaii.”

Rob was still groggy as he heard Bill explain how the doctors had to amputate part of his muscle and reconstruct his knee. Rob did not care, he was just grateful to be alive.

“Stop avoiding your promise. I stayed alive to hear about that brown-eyed girl who stole your heart. Hey, is she meeting us in Hawaii? One look at me in a swimsuit and she might drop you like a rock.”

Bill looked at him with a puzzled look, almost pissed off. Then he cracked a smile and they both started to laugh.

“Tell me about your girl American. You owe me, remember?” Rob called Bill out for avoiding his promise.

“Man, I know what I promised and I gave you my word. I was just warming you up for that side of my life.”

Rob was as excited as a kid in a candy store, he was dying to hear all about her. Rob pulled himself up and fluffed his pillow. He did not care what was happening in the rest of the world; this was his moment. Now Bill had to tell his secrets and no one was going to stop him.

Bill pulled up a chair and sat between Rob’s hospital bed and the huge picture window. Bill could see the atrium, the fountain and the park across the street.

“Hey, who did you pay off to have such nice accommodations? They put me in a closet between the broom and the mop bucket. I know who has the real pull around here.” Rob and Bill then started to laugh.

“I said I would tell you, and I was just getting one last rise out of you. Well, I guess I should start from the beginning so you don’t get too confused. I had been married to Patricia for almost 14 years. We were both in the military and had lots in common. I thought we had a pretty nice life for a long time. We were married, traveling, and having fun. She started spending more time at the spa, with her girls, and drinking. Then, Patricia decided to take a deployment abroad and broaden her resume. I thought it would be good for us and that once she came home we would start our family. I had a pretty good thing going. I was stationed in North Carolina and could travel anywhere at any time. I got us a furnished house near the base. I bought her a jeep and secured her a permanent position with training. I was working with data analysis and intelligence. I thought it was a win for us. 'Our next big step' like Patricia would tell me in her letters, calls, and emails. She came home and almost immediately I did not recognize her.  Patricia had become Patty or Pat. She was always hostile, irritable, unpredictable, and angry. I tried to speak to her, but all I would get was grunts, shouts, and even stuff thrown in my direction. I did not know what was going on or what I did to her. I asked her to go to counseling but she refused. One day I came home and found the house empty. Brother, when I say empty, Patty or Pat had taken everything, even the ice trays. All my stuff was packed and sent to the base with a note that read,

**"You are an idiot and I hate you. While I was gone I discovered that I was just wasting my life attached to someone as simple- minded as you. I gave you everything and you did not appreciate it. I found someone who really cares for me and we are getting married as soon as our divorce is final. Don't bother fighting it because I am pregnant with his child. I am transferring to California and hope to never see you again. You are a loser and I am a winner. Goodbye."**

I can only describe that feeling like being hit by a mortar that I never saw coming.  I kept going over and over every detail and to this day I cannot tell you where we went wrong. I thought I knew her, but I was wrong. Oh God, I was so terribly wrong. Patricia really had me fooled and all I could do was hit rock bottom.

I tried for months to back track and figure out what happened. Then I got really angry and started to drink. Man that was not drinking it was attempted drowning, with Jack Daniels.  I could not consume enough or fast enough to escape my reality or haunting memories. I hated my simple-minded self, the self who allowed her to rip my heart out. During one of those drunken stupors, I found myself cutting at my chest. I looked in the mirror and got scared.  I said, "Stop that! You are better than that. Get up and move." I cleaned myself up and started hitting the gym every day and soon enough my rage turned into fuel. In some things Patricia was right. I had been standing still too long. Don't get me wrong. I was lonely and many a night I found myself in the company of a pretty stranger. Random one night stands. You know the type: blond, or brunette with long legs, and tight abs. Overall a nice body but no real connection to the world.  Soon enough, I found myself bored and I knew I wanted more out of life.

After some soul searching I decided I needed to move and go home. I requested a transfer to Colorado. I reached out to my Dad and we got the ranch on the border between the Colorado and Wyoming Region. It is a beautiful place and the right place for me to be. We got about 100 acres and the land is just flourishing. I got Pops settled in and started looking at my life. My career was at a standstill and I needed a good bust. I thought about some sound advice from former Commanders and they were all in agreement: I should look into some type of Leadership Course. I was told it would look good on my resume and I might be considered for a commission.

Looking for the right place to take Leadership classes was not easy. I needed something that would work with my heavy travel schedule. It took a bit of time, but I found a suitable program designed for both law enforcement as well as the military. I was pretty stoked because it was a strong program, well-accredited and overall a great choice. Rob, it was the right place for me to be. Once I got into the program I began to crush it. I ripped through all the core courses and started on my capstone project. That is when the shit got real and I had four residencies in different parts of the country plus a group project. I have always been a loner so the idea of working with a group of strangers made it worse. I thought I could outsmart the system and just get with other military guys and not worry about the civilians in the class. Boy, did I get my ass handed to me with that plan!

I logged into my class and found out the system had randomly assigned the groups. As I looked through the roster I found that five of us had military experience and that there was a lone policeman. I cannot tell you how relieved I was to see only one civilian. Don't get me wrong. I like Cops, but they think like ordinary people. They do not have the ability to assemble a combat team and work in a war zone. Well, at least that's what I thought then. I honestly believed they were like Andy Griffin who worked in Mayberry. I really did not care to learn much about what they did or how Cops handled things because I think tactics and strategy, and they on the other hand are simply reactive. You know what I mean right?"  He looked at his buddy and continued with, "Okay, I was an arrogant ass and I know it." And they both laughed hysterically until they were interrupted by a physical therapist calling for Lt. Stevens who needed to work out his leg.

"Wait, Bill, you're coming back later right? You have not told me about your girl."

Bill waved Rob off as his PT session was getting started. "I will be here later, don't you worry."

Rob was awakened by some random nurse trying to change his bedding.

"Good Morning" Rob said.

"Good Morning? Are you kidding me? Lt. Stevens, you have been sleeping all morning and most of the afternoon. You better get ready for supper soon or you will miss that as well. I will not have the doctors put me on report because you need your beauty sleep." Rob looked confused and was trying hard to remember when he had fallen asleep when the nurse piped in again, "And while we are having this pleasant conversation. Please ask your friend to come to visit you during visiting hours. I don't care if they call him Ghost or not. I can still see him and hear you two chatting all night."

"Yes, Ma'am, but where is Bill?"

"Oh, Lord, I sent him downstairs to grab you a snack and coffee to wake you up. He should be back in a few hours unless he disappeared like a spirit." Between her rattling and shaking, she threw Rob a nice big smile that warmed his heart.

"Nurse, how long was I out?"

"Sir you had a bit of a panic attack, we had to medicate you so you would not damage your knee. You slept for about 15 hours, but, don't worry, your body needed it. You are recovering nicely and look, your friend is here." She pointed to Bill who was standing in the doorway holding a huge tray filled with snacks and drinks.

"So Sleeping Beauty, welcome back. How was your nap? Don't look at me that way. I did not kiss you while you were unconscious" Bill said between chuckles and smiles.

"I must look like a prince. I cannot believe that I slept for so long. What did I miss? How many times did you come over? Aren't you released yet? What is wrong with you?" Rob nailed him with rapid-fire questions.

"Wow, hold on Brother. I can answer all your questions but let's put this down and grab a seat." Bill sat the tray on the table and pulled up a chair again near the window. "I like your view, it is much better than mine. My room is drafty and small and it overlooks the ambulance bay. Remember when they took out my feet. I took a pretty bad beating and the doctors think I might have nerve damage. I am walking into your room but I run around the hospital in a wheelchair. We are waiting for a specialist to tell me how bad the damage is and what can be done for me. So you see, much like a few weeks ago kiddo, we are stuck together."

Rob pulled himself up and pushed his pillow into place and as he grabbed for his coffee and snack, then he lit into Bill, "tell me American, tell me about your girl."

Bill smiled and leaned back into his chair and began sipping his coffee. After a drink he said, "I think we left off with Leadership School. I had to put a few things on Canvas which is like a message board and people in your group will respond and comment on the post. Man, this one student always drove me crazy and not in a good way. SG007 was out to get me every time. I could not say anything without them stirring the pot. I just thought that guy wanted to press all of my buttons. And I made up my mind, the day I meet that guy I am going to punch him in the face. Soon enough I was going to get my shot."

4

**Denver**

TWO WEEKS LATER, I signed up for my first residency in Denver. Denver was perfect. I was close to home if something happened at the ranch, but it was also a nice mini-vacation since it was just a little over three hours away. I was nervous and excited all at once. But I also wanted to get that guy because he simply pissed me off. I played it a bit cheap and only booked a room for one night even though the residency was four days, Thursday to Sunday. The program was a bit expensive, but it had great reviews. I was already vested but I was not sure about this part of the program.

I got there way early too early to get into my room but with enough time to do some recon. I waited in the lobby and watched how the school staff transformed the hotel into their university. They tacked logos, filled balloons, stacked booklets, and the works. Our first meet and greet was at 0730. Lightweights! Soon after, students gathered like sheep. Networking, my ass. It was a free-for-all. Those people were stuffing their faces with free bagels, donuts, fruit, and cake. I noticed there were more men than women. And to be honest the women were nothing to write home about. I quickly filled my cup of coffee and made my way to the conference room.

Walking through the large room, I began looking for my group. I finally found the right spot near the corner, but close to the doors. Yes, near an exit and just close enough to the coffee station. After driving for almost four hours I really needed it. In a matter of minutes the room was full of people. Four men made their way to my table. I scanned them quickly and determined they were all in the service.

"Wow, I guess we all get our paychecks from Uncle Sam." Bill then noticed one member was missing and the chair was empty.

"So we are a group of five, or do you think the dude is just late?"

The guys grunted and picked their seats while half introducing themselves one at the time. I was half listening to them when one guy was going on and on about his experience which sounded just like "blah, blah, blah." Then I heard him say something about how they had sent the last member of the group to grab their orders for the project.

I was almost thinking about bolting out of the room when someone pulled out

the empty chair and sat down. As I finished my coffee and placed the cup down, I began staring at this brunette who just decided to join the group.

"Are those our assignments?" She quickly dropped five large envelopes on the table and kept scrolling through her cellphone.

"Hey did you guys read the instructions for this portion of the seminar? It looks like we have to divide the work and then come together at the end to present it. How do you guys want to do this?" she said.

The men took their packages and left the table.  "What the hell? You guys are just going to run? This just sucks ass. What? You are not going to join them? I guess there is a bar or golf game calling them. Damn it, I need this certificate and I paid for this out of my own pocket. Crap!" She stared at me and then started to look around the room. "Well the way I figure, we got a few choices: we can sit here and do all the work, we could walk away and just do our part or find another group," she said. I looked around as she grabbed her package, I said "I worked really hard to get here. Screw those guys, let's see if we can move to another table. You scope the left side and I will go right. Let's try to find a spot for both of us. No man left behind" I knew she was stressing out so I shot her a nice smile.

It was not long before I spotted a table with two open chairs. We must have been in sync because we walked to the table together. I pulled her chair out and said:

"Looks like a nice group," she smiled as she sat down. I sat and noticed everyone around us were women. "Ladies, is it possible for us to join your group?"  I then waited for the women to look up from their cell phones.

"Absolutely, we were short two," I am Neely, Kate Neely, US Navy, I'm an analyst. Kate then went on to introduce the rest of the group, "that is Natalie Porter she is a strategist with the Air Force, and Barb Andersen who works at the Pentagon. And you guys are?"

Bill cleared his throat, "Hi. I am William, Bill Young. US Army. I work with intelligence." And looked at her and said, "I don't know your name."

"Hey, thanks for taking us in. I'm Sabina Contreras Goodwin and I am a patrolman in Florida."

Kate said, "I hope you guys don't mind, but we already started talking about the assignment and divided the project according to experience. Are you guys good to work together? I mean you both seem to have strong security backgrounds. But if you want us to start over, that will be fine too."

Bill laughed out loud as he said, "I am good with that. How about you Goodwin?"

She smiled and said, "I think that is a great idea. Listen compared to the last group you guys are on point. Let's get to it."

The morning flew by and soon enough the group divided to head to the breakout sessions. Bill followed Sabina into her first session.

"Hey, are you coming to learn about strategic decisions for mass events?" Sabina asked.

"Yes, I guess so. To be honest I signed up for this residency while I was deployed. I did not have time to choose my classes. Do you mind if I shadow you for a bit?" Bill said almost in a whispered voice.

Sabina looked puzzled but she quickly replied, "Oh of course, I hope you don't get bored in this one. It is like 90 minutes. After we are done, I will show you how to download the app and you can choose the next one.  Do you know we have to take at least two breakout sessions every day?" They walked in and sat together during the session. Every few minutes Bill found himself staring at Sabina. She was pretty, and confident but what he really liked was that she seemed so easygoing.

"Wow, William I am so sorry. I did not know it was a double session. If you like I will download the app to your phone and you will not get stuck again." Sabina said in an apologetic tone.

"No way lady, I enjoyed it and learned a lot. What did you pick for tomorrow? Anything good? I am going to have to rely on you since my phone is dead. Can you show me in the morning?"

Sabina smiled and nodded. She started to walk away towards the elevator, when Bill said, "That's it? You done for today? It is still early, where are you going?"

"Nap I need a nap or a big cup of coffee. I think I'm jet lagged and I am out of fuel." Sabina said with a half-smile. She was looking tired and exhausted.

"A coffee run sounds like the right strategic move. Come on, we can just walk across the street to the coffee shop and get a donut." Bill heard himself pleading.

She laughed and it looked like her eyes twinkled for a second, "Ok soldier, but I want to eat more than a donut. We can start taking a few of our pictures for the presentation as well," she said.

Sabina reached for the door when she saw Bill slam his hand over her shoulder and pushed the door shut. Sabina looked shocked when she heard him say,

"Excuse me, but my father raised me to be a man and a gentleman. I will be getting the doors for you. All the doors. I might also pull out chairs. Just don't freak out." Sabina looked surprised, but then chuckled.

As the wind hit Sabina, she realized the temperature had dropped and she was not well dressed for the weather. "Oh Lord, I thought it was April. I mean its spring, right? Spring should not be this cold!"

Bill smiled warmly and said, "Did you forget you came to Denver? In Colorado it snows until the end of May. You want to cancel coffee or go for it? Bill could not say it fast enough as Sabina was darting across the street.

Bill and Sabina had a great time chatting about their lives and careers. They spent hours talking about things they liked, hated, and also their hopes and dreams. Bill caught himself staring at Sabina as she talked about Florida. She looked animated when she talked about her adventures in the Sunshine State. Bill got embarrassed when she noticed how fixed and intensely he was looking at her. "And now you tell me something about you. I have been rambling on and on. You better take your turn before I start talking again."

Bill was smiling from ear to ear as he was sipping his coffee. "Someone thought it was a good idea to nickname me the Ghost. It was not my idea but the name stuck. You see, my job is to meet with insurgents who are willing to sell us intelligence. I carry duffle bags with millions across the streets of Baghdad and no one seems to notice me. I meet in plain sight and buy information. It is crazy to think about it. I get locations, operations, and strategies all in exchange for good old American dollars. They really hate us in the Middle East but love our cash. It is simply nuts when you think about it. The troops call me the Ghost because I move from place to place without being captured, shot at, or killed. I had a couple of close calls, but I am still here."

Sabina looked at her watch and noticed it was past 10 PM. "Hey, this is nice, but we need to get some sleep. Are you ready to go back?"

Bill stood up and pulled her chair out, "Alright Officer Goodwin, let's get you back."

"I meant to tell you it's Contreras. I am dropping the Goodwin; that is my ex-husband's last name. It's a long story. For another time maybe? Today has been fun and I just don't feel like bringing the mood down. Ready?" Sabina replied as she reached for the door handle.

Once again Bill would not allow her to open the door. This time he gently opened the door and placed his hand on the small of her back. "Don't run across the street please, it just snowed and you might slip." Sabina looked confused when she felt the cold breeze running through her body. She wanted to run across the street, but as soon as she took a step forward her heel broke. She felt herself falling when Bill caught her.

"Crap! My shoe! My heel broke. Why did I think I could pull off heels? I'm just an idiot."

Bill grabbed her and lifted her like a sack of potatoes over his shoulder. "Really. A dead man carry? You have got to be kidding me William. I am wearing a skirt."

"You want to argue or go inside where it's warm." Bill scolded her, "Hold on. We are almost there. I will take you across the street and see if the gift shop has a pair of slippers for you." "Bill, I don't care, just get me inside; I am freezing out here."

They walked into the lobby just to see that the gift shop was closed. There was no one at the reception desk and the place looked pretty empty. "New plan. I will get you to your room and check your ankle." Bill pressed the elevator button and while he waited he could not help but check out her legs. Amazing. He thought her legs were muscular but sensual; Sabina had a very sexy body. Her curves were both alluring and mysterious. He could feel her body tensing up and he snapped out of his head, "Which is your floor?" Bill questioned as the elevator began to move up.

"Tenth. I am on the tenth floor. It is room 1020. You don't understand how embarrassing this is. I hope no one sees us. I swear I look like a sack of potatoes." Sabina complained until they reached the tenth floor. "Bill, it's the very last room at the end of the hallway." She then handed him her key card and Bill managed to open the door. He gently sat her down on the couch and knelt down in front of her. Sabina reached for the scrap that secured her shoe around her ankle when she felt light-headed. "Good Lord, the room is spinning" she said almost in a panic. Sabina then began to fall when Bill caught her and helped her lay down.

Sabina fainted for a few seconds and when she regained consciousness, Bill was next to her crouching on the floor. "Hey, what happened? How long was I out?" Sabina seemed confused.

"Here, drink some water, it might have been the change of altitude," Bill said in a soft tone.  Sabina sat up, "You are not that tall."

Bill let out a robust laugh, "No, Sunshine girl, you are in Colorado-the altitude affects people who are not used to it. You need to hydrate and get some rest. It is probably a combination of the altitude, dehydration, and jetlag. I'm sorry for keeping you out so late."

Sabina smiled, took a drink and began to sit-up.  "Let's check that ankle. If it needs to be iced, we need to do it right away." Bill said.

"I think I'm fine. I just need to get my shoes off. Just let me get up and move."

"Wait, let me help you. I really don't mind," Bill said as he reached for Sabina's feet. He helped her slip off the right heel and then the one that was broken on the left. He rubbed her ankle carefully inspecting it. Bill rubbed up and down and then began stroking her foot in a circular motion. Bill's mind began to drift as he felt her soft skin.

"Bill, Bill I think my ankle is okay. I don't think I sprained it. I am sure I can stand once you step back." Sabina said. Bill snapped out of it once again and in an almost embarrassed manner, he leapt to his feet.

Sabina slowly stood up and took a very unsteady step forward, "See I'm good. Nothing a good night's sleep and shower can't cure."

Bill was speechless and he began making his way to the door. Sabina quickly sat back down as if to catch her breath. "I better go, unless you need anything" Bill said.

"No, I'm good. I will just sit here for a few more minutes and drink more water. Goodnight. Wait, I will see you in the morning right? "Sabina said.

"Get some rest and grab us coffee and save our seats. You get some shut-eye."

Bill started to walk out of the room when he turned and said, "Just do me a favor before you go to sleep, secure the safety latch Okay? You can text me if you need anything. I am sure my cell phone will be charged by now." She nodded and closed her eyes as he walked into the hallway. Bill waited outside her room for a few minutes when he heard the latch being applied from inside of Sabina's room. Somehow that sound comforted him as he made his way to the elevator and towards the fourth floor.

He could smell her perfume lingering on his shoulder. He closed his eyes wondering what was happening. They only knew one another for a few hours, but they were not strangers. He was comfortable with Sabina and she seemed natural to be around. The elevator doors opened and Bill found his room. Bill heard his cell phone announcing he had a text message. 'What the Hell?' he thought, 'I can't even get a vacation from work?' Bill looked at the message it was from Sabina. He smiled as he read, "Thank you for taking me. I really appreciate it. Don't worry I latched the door and drank lots of water. Hope you are well. C U in the morning. I take my coffee black. Smiley face." Bill smiled and replied with a thumbs up Emoji and got settled in to bed.

Bill's thoughts kept racing and he was not sure how to process what was happening.  He told himself it was because he was lonely, or the residency atmosphere. Yes, that's it, he said out loud. New people getting together and all the hormones. It's like the first day of school. It will pass. But something kept bothering him and it did not help that Sabina's perfume was on his shirt and he could see her every time he closed his eyes. That is it, I am just lonely and a bit horny. I will take a cold shower and go to bed. He was somewhere between laughter and shivering as the ice cold water nailed his body. It did not take long for all those thoughts to quickly evaporate and all his body wanted was to be warm. It helped for a while, but pretty soon Bill's mind was just counting the hours to see Sabina again.

The morning finally came and it did not seem too early for Bill to get started with his day. He told himself last night was a fluke and today was a new day. He would concentrate on the tasks at hand and not on the women or better yet a woman in particular.  Bill walked out of his room mission-oriented and ready for the day. He went to the coffee shop and grabbed two black medium coffees and walked into the convention center. It was just a few minutes after 7:00 A.M. and to his surprise Sabina and all the other ladies were sitting at their designated spot working on their laptops. "Good Morning Team," Bill said.

Kate looked up for her work with a smile, "everyone had a similar idea by bringing two coffees. Now that we are all caffeinated, let's get to work, shall we?" Barb looked a bit distracted and it looked like she had been crying. "Barb, do you want to speak to Goodwin about your situation?" Kate asked quietly.

"Yes, I think it might be a good idea. Do you have a minute or two, Goodwin?" Sabina stood up and walked towards the door with Barb.

Barb took a deep breath and stared out of the huge picture window. "My son is at George Washington University and last night he got into a bit of trouble. He was caught drinking on campus and he is looking at expulsion. He called me last night after he was released by campus police. I am not trying to excuse him but I do not know how to handle this situation. Bo is a good kid but we lost his father five years ago. My husband was a Rescue Swimmer for the Coast Guard. He jumped in to save a fisherman off the coast of South Carolina. They both perished and Bo was devastated. I became both mother and father for Bo, but now I do not seem like I am strong enough. I found work in D.C. with the Pentagon and Bo seemed to be handling things. Well at least that is what I thought until I got the call last night. He wants to go to Law School and I am not sure if this will keep him out. I do not know what to do. Can you help me figure this out?" Barb pleaded.

Sabina took a deep breath, "Wait, your son was on campus when he got caught drinking right? That sounds like the campus police are handling it in-house. Your Bo can ask for a hearing and maybe do community service. I would consult an attorney in the area if they are not willing to work with you guys. Honestly, Barb each state handles things differently, but most of them are not willing to throw a college kid's future away. In Florida, as long as they were not driving we give them a citation similar to a traffic ticket. A good attorney turns that into a nothing charge and some community hours. He will be alright as long as you both stay on top of it all," Sabina said. She then focused on Barb, "listen, Bo will be alright I am sure. You guys just need to talk. I am sure you will figure it out. But if you need anything please let me know. I am here if you need to talk."

Barb looked at Sabina with kindness and replied, "Thank you so much."

As the women began walking back into the room, Barb stopped dead in her tracks, and asked, "What is going on between you and Bill? He seems to be very much into you. You guys having something of a romance? What? You don't see it? Bill is into you and now the question is are you into him?" Sabina looked shocked with the turn of the conversation. Barb, who can only be described as a short pear-shaped woman with long stringy hair said, " he is hot and if I was a bit younger and taller, maybe skinnier, I would go for him. Clearly, he has gone for you, but I would give you a run for your money." Both women began to laugh till they almost cried. "I saw you guys last night near the elevator. He was carrying you like a bag of flour right over his shoulder. Never did I wish to be young and pretty or be a sack of flour."

Sabina started to laugh again and said, "Listen, you got it all wrong. Bill is my friend and he was only helping me. My heel broke and well, Bill is a gentleman. He thought it was the best solution to get me to my room safely. We are not in any type of romance." Sabina then exhaled and waited for Barb to respond.

Barb patted her hand and said, "Kiddo, I work at the Pentagon I know all about everyone in our group. Master Sergeant William Michael Young is a good guy. He has been through some bad deployments but he is really good at this job. He has saved countless of our soldiers. They call him' Ghost' because he can navigate between regions without anyone noticing him. You my Dear on the other hand, have been working tirelessly at your agency for years. Both of you are divorced and from what I know neither of you are dating anyone."

"Well Barb, you really know a lot about us. It is a bit scary to know the Pentagon has access to our deepest secrets" Sabina replied.

"I do not mean to scare you, but I am a naturally curious person which makes me perfect for my job. I checked on everyone because I did not want to be surprised. My job requires a top security clearance and I need to know who I am working with at all times. You guys snuck up on me when you joined the group, but I did my homework. You guys are good people."

The women returned to the group and joined the rest of the team. Natalie whispered to Bill, "See, your girl is back."

Bill looked at her puzzled and responded, "What are you talking about?" Natalie went on to say, "Don't worry your secret's safe with me. I see how you watch her and follow her when she is gone. You seem to be getting close. Close is nice right?"

Bill winked and pulled the chairs so Barb and Sabina could sit. Bill said, "You guys good?" Both women nodded and sat down.

Quickly, Kate took the lead and said, "Alright team, it seems like we are looking well. As each of you upload your portion to the folder, I will paste it together. So here are some notes: Barb we need more data regarding possible overseas threats, Bill I need your experience with routes, and exit strategies. Oh and Sabina I need more photos and first responder support. I checked with the proctor and we have a nice long break before our next session. We are looking at a four-hour window. So go out and do your thing and enjoy the break. Denver is a beautiful town, but don't wander too far."

Bill looked around and it seemed like most if not all the groups were dismissing. As he stood up he noticed the ladies were bolting for the door except for Sabina, who was searching something on her cellphone. "What are you Googling? Anything good?" Bill asked.

"You are going to laugh but I don't have another pair of heels. So I am looking for a shoe shop close-by" Sabina responded without looking up for her phone.

"Seriously, you need to buy heels?" Bill said laughing.

"Well, I only packed one pair and one pair of boots, which is what I am wearing. I do not think the board would appreciate me presenting with cowboy boots. So I need a pair of heels," she said while she stood up and started walking towards the door.

"Wait, I will go with you. We can get you some shoes and finish our project at the same time if you would like the company," Bill said.

Sabina went to grab the door handle and once again she saw Bill's hand blocking it. " I told you my father raised a man who is also a gentleman. I will get the door for you." Sabina smiled as they walked out together.

The wind hit her like a cold pie to the face. Sabina managed to say, "Damn, I did not think it was this cold in April. The store is only a few miles away so we can walk or take the trolley. What do you think?"

Bill responded, "Trolley definitely. You will enjoy it a bit more." As they hopped on, Bill positioned himself behind Sabina." You better hold on to this rail.  Things rock a bit and it breaks hard." Sabina tried to reach the handhold but her five feet four inches failed her. She took another few steps forward and found a nice spot with a rail which she grabbed tightly. Bill did not take long to reposition himself behind her to block off the elements. Bill noticed how perfectly Sabina's stature fit his build. He could stand behind her and her head reached his shoulder. He could smell her spell-bounding perfume. Bill noticed her long wavy hair that reached down halfway to her back. He started to lose himself as he examined the small curve of her back. She was wearing a bomber jacket and a sweater which layered to some form fitting jeans. Bill could not help but wonder why she was single. Or was she? He didn't really know.

As the street car took off, snow began to fall and cover Sabina's hair, face and eye lashes. She instinctively raised her head to catch a few snowflakes. When she turned she could see Bill sticking his entire head out through the open window. "You okay Sunshine Girl? Have you ever seen snow before? Don't tell me it's your first time?" Bill teased her. All Sabina could do was nod in agreement. "Okay then we need to celebrate this. Come on, let's get off this thing and walk. The snow will stop soon and the sun will melt it. Come on, let's jump off here." The trolley stopped and Bill reached out his hand to help Sabina off the platform.

Bill placed his hand on the small curve of Sabina's back and they walked together silently, just enjoying each other's company when Sabina came to a dead stop. She stood frozen in front of a boutique store window and she began to smile. "Look Bill, this is the shoe store. Well it's not just a shoe store but they should have what I need. Do you mind if I go in? I will be superfast, I promise" she said with excitement.

Bill looked confused at her pleas, "Sunshine, you take your time. Find what you need or want. I will just enjoy watching you."

"Really? My ex would have been flipping out." Sabina said while reaching for the door. She then turned to Bill and said, "I'm sorry. I will wait for you to open the door. I am not used to it" Bill laughed as they walked into the shop.

Bill watched Sabina pick up a black pair of heels similar to the ones from the other night. He watched as she walked through the boutique enjoying all items on display. She focused on a shawl which had a Native American plaid pattern. Sabina tried it on as the salesperson walked towards her saying, "You have exquisite taste. That is a unique piece. One of a kind made here in Colorado by a local artist. It is handmade and painted. You would be foolish not to buy it.”

Sabina looked at and asked, “How much is it?”

The salesperson said, “$450.00”

“Well, it is worth it, and I wish I could afford it” she said, as she handed it back to the associate. “Please tell the artist it was an honor just to try it on. An amazing piece of art really.”

“Look,” the salesperson said, “There are more items near the back you might like. Good stuff, your style and in clearance. Come let’s find something you will love. Tell your boyfriend we are walking back here.”

Quickly, Sabina found herself trying on a spaghetti-strapped dress that matched her new heels. She walked out of the dressing room to find Bill patiently sitting in a chair near the mirror.

“I told your boyfriend to have a seat. We ladies need a few minutes to look beautiful.”

“Ma’am, he is not my boyfriend. He is my friend who I hope will give his honest opinion. So Bill, what do you think? I’m going to a wedding next week. Do you think I can pull this off?”

Bill stood up and inspected Sabina from head to toe. “Wow, you look amazing and that dress fits you like a glove.”

The sales woman walked closer to Sabina and said, “You might need to alter it an inch or two since you are short in stature.” Bill nodded no and whispered ‘You look very pretty’.

Sabina ran into the dressing room and changed back. “Bill, I trust you so I will take it.” She handed the items to the associate who said she was happy to ship the dress to her house free of charge.

“Great day right? I got to see snow, did some shopping, and took lots of photos. What a nice day. Thank you Bill. I haven’t felt this way in a long time. Do you want to stop for anything? We still have plenty of time.”

“Coffee sounds good. Even better with a warm donut” Bill suggested.

Sabina agreed, "Yes, but my treat. Alright? You have done so much for me. If you get the door, I will pay the tab. Yes? It's settled then. Come on, there is a bakery right here."

"No, Sabina, we can't go there. Let's do the donut shop across the street." Bill placed his hand on her waist and off they went.

"What gives? Bakery. Donut Shop. Same difference." Sabina questioned.

"Your Cop skills are lacking here in Pot Land. That bakery sells only marijuana-infused goodies. Colorado legalized it last election, but if that is your thing I will call you Amsterdam and not Sunshine Girl," Bill replied.

"Holy shit Bill, I did not realize how easy it was to buy dope in this state. I smelled it all over, but I did not think it was so open."

"Yep, not my thing since we get drug tested all the time. I can imagine you as well" Bill said with a huge smile on his face.

"I can just imagine going to Internal Affairs telling them I ate a loaded brownie in Denver" she said as she started to laugh.

# 5

## Spilled Perfume

After coffee and a snack they headed to the hotel. Bill opened the door and led Sabina inside. "Hey, do you mind if I stop at the Bellhop Station. I dropped my luggage this morning. I just need to check how late they are open so I can grab my stuff tonight and head home," Bill said. Sabina watched while Bill talked to the receptionist and seemed confused by his decision to head home.

When Bill walked back to her, Sabina seemed quiet and not herself. "What's up? What did I miss? We are not late to meet with the ladies are we? We should still have 30 minutes" Bill asked.

"No, I just got used to you. I mean I just did not think you were heading home early." Sabina responded softly.

Bill smiled, "No Sunshine I am just a Dumb Ass. I booked the room for one night and when I checked this morning nothing was available. There is some other thing going on here like a Little Miss Something Beauty competition and I was also just informed there is some type of Karate thing going on as well, so no rooms in the area at all. I have to either sleep in my truck which I don't mind except for the crazy moms watching me like I was a pervert or hoof it home back and forth."

Sabina smiled, "Why don't you ask someone if you can just crash with them?"

Bill said, "Well I thought of that, but the only service guys we hung out with are Assholes. I guess I could see if one of my team members would let me sleep on their floor."

"Or you could just grab your bag and follow me" Sabina said in a very coy tone of voice.  Bill grabbed his duffle bag and she led the way into the elevator. "Ok, you will have to promise not to tell anyone that I am the winner of the Executive Suite raffle, " Sabina insisted. "I got the notification last month and I don't believe the American Military University meant to make me the winner. I just applied because it is open to all participants. I was shocked to see I got it" she said as she pushed the door open. "I was sure you noticed the other night when you were here."

Bill looked around and said, "No, not really I guess I was focused on something else." He dropped his bag and replied, "I am good sleeping on the couch and I can shower inside of the gym."

She started to laugh, "Bill, it's the Executive Suite just walk past the bar and open that door." Bill looked amazed at the size of the room. There was a living room area, a bar, a dining room area and the most spectacular view of the Rocky Mountains. He made his way to the door and walked into a king- size bed, a closet, private bathroom, and his own entrance which led into the hallway.

"Man, Sunshine, you are one lucky woman. This place is amazing and huge" Bill said with excitement.

"Does it suit you? You will stay then?" Sabina questioned.

"Hell yes. I am in Heaven. But let me pay for half please. I would not feel right mooching off you. I can't believe how kind you are to me. I am still shocked at the size of this room."

"Well we will deal with the expenses later. To be honest from what I was told I paid for the regular room rate and the University forked over the money for the upgrade. I would not know what it is until I check out. But I do want to ask you for a favor or two. I don't want anyone to know you are here sharing the room. You can use your private entrance, and I would prefer it if you do not bring anyone to our room. I am a very private person and I just don't want gossip or drama. So if you hook up with someone, can you do it somewhere else?" Sabina said in a stern manner.

"Listen, Sunshine, you are doing me a huge favor and like I said my father raised a man and a gentleman. I would never just hook up with someone for the sake of hooking up. Honestly, I have been there and done that. I hated that guy. Secondly, I respect the rules and you will not have to worry about me. And finally, I promised not to snitch about the sweet suite you scored because you are a genius."

Sabina still looked very serious when she said, "I promise to follow the rules as well. Good?" "Of course, now let's head downstairs before Kate sends out her posse for us."

"Hey you two, did you get everything accomplished today?" Kate questioned. "Yes, mission accomplished. And I want to report that Sabina Goodwin got to see snow for her very first time."

Bill looked at Sabina and said, "Wait, you are SG007 from the classroom chats?"

"It took you long enough son," Barb piped in with laughter and continued, "this girl has given you a run for your money all semester and then some. I was wondering when it would click Mr. Army Intel." The group started to laugh while Bill stood stoic and speechless.

"I swore you were going to punch me in the nose the first day we met. And I was surprised that you didn't" Sabina said.

Bill started to laugh, "Man, you got me. You got me good. I got distracted with everything else I forgot about the jerk in class. Sorry Sunshine girl, but you really got under my skin."

"Wait! I was just telling you how civilian life works and everything is military tactics." "Oh no, we will not have this dissension among my ranks" Kate said, "Our project is complete and up for review. You two kiss and make up. We need you guys tonight for the mixer. Dancing, singing, and lots of drinking."

Barb got up and wiggled her stocky short body in front of Bill and said, "You Sir will be escorted by three very prepared and strong women. You better be up to the challenge." The group busted out in laughter as they walked out together into the lobby.

"So change your clothes, and take a nap. I will see everyone at 7:00 PM at the event" Kate instructed.

The group disbanded and everyone went their separate ways. Sabina noticed that Bill was on his cellphone and it looked like a serious call. She decided to let him be and she made her way to her side of the room. I will text him later, she thought, just to make sure things are good. She went into her room and took a cat nap. It was so refreshing to rest and then get ready to enjoy a few hours of free time. Around 6:45 she received a text from Bill, "hey do you want to meet at the elevator or living room?"

Sabina replied, "I will c u in the living room. We can head down 2gether."

He walked into the room to find Sabina gazing out the window. As he walked into the room she said, "The Mountains look amazing. I wish I had enough time to go see them. You are so lucky you are able to look at this view every day."

Bill replied, "Not every day but the days I am here I do love it. I got a call today and it looks like I will not be seeing the Rockies for a while. I got new orders today. I guess I am headed back to the Sandbox."

Sabina reached for his hand, "When are you deploying? Soon?"

"I am not sure; within the next six months. I told my Commander I was working through this Leadership Program and he agreed to let me stay until I complete it. So I guess you might be stuck with me for the next two residencies."

"I am glad we met and we are friends. This is nice." She said,

"Yes it is. Are you ready?" He replied.

They met the other ladies outside of the lobby and walked together to the makeshift disco inside of one of the side rooms. Lights, smoke machine and music banging.

"Look," said Barb of the karaoke, "I love karaoke especially after a few drinks." The group found a table as Barb started signing everyone up for different songs. "Come on you guys, we are up. **Purple Rain** by Prince." Barb yelled over everyone and took her shot of whiskey. She then grabbed Bill's hand and said, "The Army has never let me down." They got on stage and Barb started belting out the lyrics as Bill attempted to follow along. It did not take long for him to catch up to Barb's mood and soon enough he was all into it. When they were done, the crowd went wild as Barb took her bows. "See I told you guys I love this stuff. Bartender, another round on me."

"Barb, you don't need to pay for the drinks. We have been getting drinks for free because of the Ghost. Once the guys found out that he was here we got an open tab. Man, you are a lucky charm" Kate said. She then continued by asking, "Hey, where did Natalie go? She is killing me guys. We agreed to room together, but last night she hooked up with some guy and I ended up sleeping in the tub. Now look, she is hanging on to another guy and I know I am going to be looking for a place to crash" Kate complained while slamming down another shot.

Bill and Sabina looked at one another and before they could say anything, Barb blurted out, "I did not find anyone to be my residency honey. You can sleep in my room. I got double beds." She then rubbed Bill's arm and said "how about another one handsome?" Bill smiled as he was nursing his beer. "Come on, let's go pick out our song." She took Bill's hand and led him away.

Kate kept drinking shots and as they were brought to the table until Sabina said to her, "Kate I know it's none of my business, but are you alright?"

Kate began to slur as she responded, "I hate the fact that Natalie is so careless with herself." Kate then went on to say in a loud tone, "she is just inconsiderate, you know what I mean. She is bringing drunk guys into my room and I don't know, what if they get confused and slip into my bed. Plus she is messy and I really cannot stand her."

Sabina tried to comfort her by saying, "You know we are all broken in one way or another. We are just put together by tape and glue. Natalie might just be lost, she is spilled perfume. No excuse for her choices, but I get it. You need to be safe, so go and stay with Barb tonight. Besides, it's our last night.

"What is Spilled Perfume?" Kate asked.

"Like the song by Pam Tillis, **Spilled Perfume**.  One night stands." Sabina responded.

"Let's go hangout with the rest of the gang and have some water now" Sabina insisted to Kate.

They walked over towards the stage and Barb was gesturing to join them. Sabina pulled Kate on stage and they all sang along to Barry Manilow's **Copacabana**.

"You guys need to sing one." Barb said as she handed the mic to Sabina.

"We need a drink." She pulled Kate off the stage as the music began.

Bill started singing, "Picture perfect memories scattered all around the floor reaching for the phone cause I can't fight it anymore."

Sabina turned towards Bill with the mic in her hand," And I wonder if I ever cross your mind for it happens all the time."

Bill leaned over to Sabina and said, "Wow, you sound amazing."

She smiled and kept singing much like a professional.  After the song ended they went back to hanging out. Bill got another text message and told the group he had to end his night early. He headed to his room confident that the ladies would take care of one another. A few hours later he heard a loud noise coming from Sabina's room. He looked at the clock and saw it was 2:30 AM. He did not want to intrude but wanted to know if she was alright. Bill walked through the living room space and gently tapped on the door.

"Hey Sunshine, are you good?"

"Come on Bill. I'm just a klutz. I tripped on the suitcase and hit the floor."

Bill walked in to find Sabina sitting on the floor between her bed and closet.

"I thought I should start packing, but I think the drinks got to me."

He started to help her up and sat her on the edge of the bed.  Her hair was disheveled and he gently brushed it back.  His hand caressed her check. Bill could feel the attraction between them but he knew Sabina was in no condition to do anything. Bill knew he had lots of regrets in his life and he was not going to force Sabina to be another one in his long list. So he gave her a huge smile and knelt next to her. He started to remove her shoes and then laid her over the bed. Bill walked in her closet and grabbed the extra blanket. He carefully covered her body and made sure she was comfortable.

"Hey let me get you some water and an aspirin before you knock out." Bill walked to his room and came back in a few minutes with the items. He then sat down in the chair next to her and watched her sleep for a while. Around 5:30 AM, Bill ran downstairs and came up with two strong black cups of coffee.  He checked on Sabina and she was still out and therefore he decided to let her sleep for a bit more while he hit the shower and packed his bag. He walked back into her room to find her waking up.

"Good morning, Sunshine. I thought you could use a coffee."

"How long was I out? Did you sleep in that chair all night? I am so embarrassed Bill. I am so sorry. I was with Kate and she really got wasted. I had to help Barb get her to their room, but she would not let us go without one more drink."

Bill laughed so hard that he spilled his coffee all over his shirt. "Crap that is hot. Oh my God that burns." Bill then quickly peeled off his shirt and under shirt. Sabina looked at his muscular body and she then focused on his chest. He had three or four scars covering his left side which looked like cuts of his chest and two round marks near the right side of his clavicle.  Bill caught her staring at him as he brushed off the coffee.

"I got shot here and here" He pointed to his clavicle and he stood to turn his back and said, "I got whipped pretty hard the first time I got captured and my back still tells that story." He then took a deep breath and said as he pointed to his heart, "this was me being an idiot. When my wife left I thought I could end the pain by removing my heart. Pretty dumb. "

Sabina looked at him and replied, "Nope, you carry the story of your life in outside scars while others of us have scars too deep to see. My ex used to beat me up because he thought no one would believe me or I would not report it. Pretty pathetic right? Here I am a cop arresting domestic abusers and my spouse, a cop as well, is using me as an ashtray." Sabina pulled her top up just enough to reveal a scar of cigarette burn just above her waist. "He said I was his and so branded me one night like cattle. Asshole, but even after that, I stayed for two more years. Now who is the idiot?"

Bill was speechless and kept sipping on what was left of his coffee. Sabina started to get up and looked at the clock.

"Oh my God! I better get going or we are going to be late to present our project." She rushed off to the bathroom as Bill let himself out of her room. She yelled out, "I will catch you downstairs ok?" She turned on the shower and she did not hear Bill's response. Then she got packed quickly and left her bags with the bellhop.

Sabina paid for the room in full and thought not to say anything to Bill. She then walked into the convention center to see her team waiting anxiously for her arrival.

"What's up?" she asked.

"We are progressing to the next level all thanks to you. The notes read that most of the teams did not have law enforcement or civilian approach. Because of your experience we are in line to be the first team." Kate said with pride. "I guess we move to the next lecture and then we will be dismissed until mid of April. We meet again in D.C. You guys registered right? Barb, you want to room with me?" Kate pleaded with Barb, who nodded in agreement.

Bill walked behind the group and sat in the last seat while Sabina sat on the other side. Barb kept telling him about D.C. and about the cherry blossoms that were blooming. As the speaker stopped and everyone clapped, Bill found himself tangled among several people. He looked and looked but could not spot Sabina. He walked to the receptionist desk just to discover that she had checked out and paid all the expenses. He began texting her like a mad man and then waited for her response.

"Sunshine where did you go?"

"I just got on the trolley. Trolley then train then plane to get home." She replied.

"Get off, I need to see you."

"Smiley face," she replied.

"Hop off please. I promise to get you to the airport. I promise just please hop off"

"Alright, I will. Meet you @ Taco Bell."

Bill made his way to the Taco Bell where he could see Sabina on her phone and typing like mad.

"Hey Sunshine girl, why did you escape that way? I wanted to say good bye and take you to the airport. Plus I owe you money for the room."

"Bill, we are straight. You took such good care of us; just think of it like a thank you for your service. Besides the room was prepaid no worries. We are straight. Now I just have to figure out this flight mess.  I just got a notification that I got bumped to the 8 or 10 PM flight."

"Take the 10 PM and let me show you Colorado." Bill said as he pulled out a package wrapped in butcher paper.

"What is this? You did not have to get me anything," Sabina said as she unwrapped it to reveal the lovely Native American scarf from the boutique. "I cannot accept this. It is like $500.

Don't get me wrong, it is lovely and so nice of you. But I just can't."

"Please take it. I really want you to have it. It looked amazing with your dress. Besides, when you wear that dress it will be like I am with you and that's very important to me. I really don't know how to say this to you. I am not very good at this type of stuff. I don't want to pressure you, but you are special to me. I know we were meant to be here and be friends. "And" Bill stopped, "And I don't want to scare you away. I want to do the right thing, Babe. "

Sabina looked at him and said, "I don't scare easily. I just want to be a cautious with my heart. I really like this. I like us. This is really nice. Are you okay taking it slow for a bit? I will push my flight as long as you promise to get me to airport on time and we get some food." They headed towards Bill's truck and began their adventure.

Once in the truck, Bill thought about taking her to his ranch, but he knew the clock was against them. "I want to show you my place, but we don't have enough time. Next time, if you are game."

"Bill, I would love to see your ranch. It sounds wonderful. You said you had horses and cattle?"

"Horses, I have a horse ranch. It's about 100 acres with a couple of barns and two homes. One for me and like a mother-in-law cabin for my Dad. I didn't want him to lose his independence, but I really needed him close to me. He really is the one that runs things day to day.  Dad buys the horses, handles their care, and shows them. He also built a few cabins throughout the property. I don't mind, it's what he loves to do. I just enjoy that he loves it so much."

"That is fascinating. I would love to see the place, but I don't want to be rushed."

"I know, let's go toward the Rocky Mountain National Park. You will love it since the area encompasses a spectacular range of mountains. There are meadows, trails, creeks, and it really is one of my favorite places in the world. I want to share it with you if you wish."

Sabina smiled and nodded while she secured her seatbelt. She added an alert to her cell phone and put it into her pocket. Now she was just going to enjoy the moment and not worry about her flight.

Bill started pointing out places as they drove north straight to the mountain range. Sabina was hypnotized by his descriptions and explanations of Colorado. He explained how the state was discovered and all the Native American tribes that called the state home. Sabina enjoyed learning all about Bill's home state. They stopped here and there for coffee and snacks and even souvenirs. Sabina took a lot of photos and sent them to Bill's phone as they went. Bill pulled over almost at the top of the mountain range. The view was simply spectacular. The sky seemed to be almost reachable. The area seems to be desolated but majestic. Sabina felt her breath being taken away as she stepped out of the cab of the truck.

"It looks like a painting. I can't believe this place is real. My God it is simply breathtaking. Thank you so much for bringing me here. I would have never made it up here without you."

Bill smiled and walked towards Sabina. He placed his arm around her waist and led her towards the rail to see the rest of the view. He then took out his cell phone and snapped a selfie.  He then turned his attention to absorbing Sabina's reaction as she took in the scenery. He waited a few minutes until she seemed to be ready to speak.

"This is the place I come to when I need to speak to God. I know it sounds cheesy but this is my special place. I don't know why but I wanted you to be here with me. I am so glad that I met you. Sometimes I think God just puts us in the right place at the right time. You SG007, I was destined to meet you here in Denver. All the stars aligned for you and me, and I don't want to mess this up.  This is nice and I just don't want to scare you away."

Sabina felt a chill and she began to shiver. Bill reached for her and pulled her body closer to his to keep her warm. He bent down a bit and whispered, "Sunshine I am dying to kiss you, but I don't want to mess this up. If you don't want me to, I will just hold you or get you a jacket and back off."

Sabina looked into his eyes and their lips locked. It was a passionate kiss that seemed to stop time.

"I like this, whatever it is. I just want to take it slow to see where we are going. Are you good with that?" Sabina asked.

"I can wait for you or us. I just want you to be comfortable and feel safe. I want to get to know you and I want you to get to know me. I am hopeful that you will let me get to know you. And if at the end we are just friends, I am good with that too."

Sabina smiled and took Bill's arm, "I am good right now. I am happy with you at this moment."

Bill pulled her a bit closer and said, "I am happy with you at this moment and this moment is all I need." They walked off and explored more of the area. It seemed like time was against them and it kept escaping them. Soon enough Sabina's alarm went off and she confirmed her flight. Bill was sad as he started driving towards the airport. They spent the little time they had left together talking, laughing, and even lip-syncing to music as Bill drove them back towards the airport.

"I am going to have a hard time letting you go," Bill said as he opened the truck door.

"Bill we have to get back to our lives, to our reality." Sabina replied.

Once they got there, he found it difficult to step out of the truck; he wanted her to stay.

"I really don't want to say goodbye to you Sunshine. We had such a good day, a good week, and a good time" he said as shut the door. Ever the gentleman, Bill rushed open to Sabina's door.

"I have to get back to work and get ready for our next adventure. It is only a couple of weeks. Like two weekends really and then we will see one another in Barb's town," Sabina said while trying not to become too emotional.

"Will you send me pictures of you in that dress?" Bill asked in a flirtatious manner.

"I really wish you were going with me. I hate those types of things, especially by myself. I have to sing at that wedding, but I really don't want to go. It's the extended family. Since my parents died, they only call when they need something. To add insult to injury they love my ex-husband Steven. They know we are divorced, but they still ask about him. I really wish you were my plus-one. Those people drive me crazy. Sorry."

"I wish I was going too, but I have to check on a military base before I deploy. I have to pick my team and check out some equipment. If not, I would love to go. I really want to see you in that dress again." Bill said.

They walked hand in hand through the airport doors and made their way to the departing area.

"Well, I'm going to walk you to the security gate if you are good with that." Bill insisted. Bill gave her a big, long, warm hug. Sabina could feel his chiseled body all over and she had a hard time letting go. Finally, she pulled away and he once again brushed her hair back. He  caressed her cheek and gently kissed her face. Bill then whispered, "I will see you in D.C. with all the cherry blossoms."

"I see Barb talked to you as well about her D.C." Sabina said as they both started to laugh.

"Listen, we can text and call. We can video chat or FaceTime. It's only for a couple of weeks." Sabina said. They walked to the security gate and Bill reluctantly handed Sabina her suitcase.

"See you soon," Sabina said while giving Bill a hug.

"Hey Sunshine, if you need me I'm just a phone call away. I still want to see you in that dress." Bill responded.

Sabina then reached for his face and gave him a kiss on his cheek and walked into the line. Bill waited as she made her way through the sections and then disappeared into the abyss of the airport lobby.  Bill hated to say goodbye, but he told himself they would be together soon. Bill got into his truck and headed to his ranch. Four hours later, he got a smiley face text telling him Sabina landed and she too was headed home.

Bill texted, "I am so glad you made it. Call me later good night Sunshine"

Bill was checking on his horses, drinking his first cup of coffee for the day when he got his first call from Sabina. They talked for hours about everything. Bill was happy to share his life on the ranch and his horses. Sabina then shared about her life in Florida. She told him about her small farm where she had three cows and a donkey. Bill was surprised to learn Florida was the second largest producer of beef in the United States. She explained how she rescued Mr. Pepe, her donkey and how donkeys kill snakes. Bill was amazed to learn how much they had in common. He longed to speak to her and always hated to hang up. Soon enough, it was Friday and Sabina was getting ready for the wedding. She dialed Bill and was excited to show off her dress. She waited anxiously for him to answer. She had told him to expect a call around three because she would have to be at the church by four. Sabina looked in the mirror one last time to ensure that Bill would be impressed.

# 6

## The Wedding

SABINA TOOK ONE last look at herself in the mirror. Her new satin, spaghetti-strap,  sexy ruched cocktail dress fit her body like a glove. She wore her hair up in a messy bun with sapphire pins that sparkled. Sabina wondered if the dress was too tight but Bill seemed to love it.  She wore minimal accessories because she wanted to show off her shawl. She was a bit stressed because she was not looking forward to seeing her extended relatives, but they were family. She wished Bill would be there with her, but at least she felt the comfort that they would soon be together. As she took one last spin she heard a wolf whistle,

"Hey Sunshine, you look amazing. I love the spins" Bill said.

"Oh my Lord, I did not know we had connected. I didn't know you could see me already! But okay, how do I look?"

"Sunshine, you look like a rock star. I can't believe I am not there with you. But I am not sure if you would get out the door with you looking that hot" Bill said.

"Well, I have to sing a song at the ceremony and another at the reception. As soon as I'm done I will call you. Bill, I would rather stay home and enjoy your company than deal with those people" Sabina admitted.

"Don't worry you will knock them dead. Don't worry about your family. We cannot choose our family. Go do your thing and then call me. I will be here waiting. I promise I will be here waiting for you to call me."

"Bill, I am worried because I am sure they invited Steven, my ex and he is a jackass. I really want to cancel" Sabina said.

"No way! Don't give him the satisfaction. You go sing your heart out and I will be waiting for you Sunshine" Bill encouraged her. Sabina pulled herself together and promised to video chat on her way home.

Sabina was filled with encouragement and she thought to herself, William is so right; we can't choose our family but that should not change who we are. She thought how nice it would be to go to the church and light a candle in memory of her parents. She was sure it was their love that sent William her way. Sabina walked into the church and she was still feeling a bit nervous. She thought she would send Bill a quick wink to see if he was really waiting for her. Then suddenly her phone rang with an unknown number,

"Hello," she said.

"Sunshine, are you good?" Bill's voice sounded so far away.

"Where are you? I thought you were traveling today from base to base?"

"I am but I got your text. Right now we are about to leave Georgia. I only have a few seconds. Are you good?"

"I'm good," she said.

"Knock them dead I will " and the call disconnected.

Sabina stared at the phone for a minute hoping he would call back but he did not. She put her phone in her clutch purse and walked in. The church was breath-taking, filled with white and pink flowers. There were jewels marking each section with the Bride and Groom sections lit up. Sabina did not know the groom so she made her way to the Bride's side. Soon enough crowds of people started to enter including her Uncle Paco, her mother's brother, her Aunt Isabel, and cousin, Martina. Paco had taken over Sabina's father's bakery after his death.

"Oh, Princess, look! It's your cousin, the Cop Baby." He walked to her and gave her a fake kiss on the cheek.

"Where is your husband? You did not come here alone to embarrass us again did you?" questioned Isabel.

"Hi, Saby, look at you and that knock-off dress. I will ask Sophia if they have a Choir robe to cover you up." added Martina.

"No, I look fine. I checked with Sophia and she approved the dress months ago. I am here by myself Tio Paco, because you guys know Steven and I are divorced. So, I will thank you to stop fussing over me and go check on the bride" Sabina said.

"Steven is family, Mijita. You know we love him. I made sure he was invited to the wedding and he promised me he would be here" Paco said.

"I don't care if he is here or not. Today is not about him or me or you. It is Sophia's day. I will go over there until it's my turn to sing. Enjoy the ceremony" Sabina said while she walked to hide behind the altar.

"Papy, I really cannot stand her. I can't believe she was married to such a wonderful man like Steven and now they're divorced." Martina commented as they made their way to their seats.

Sabina watched the ceremony intensely waiting for her cue. She loved Sophia. Sophia's mother was her aunt on her mother's side. They came from Cuba together and once here Sabina's mother met her father and soon married. Her Aunt Jimena waited to marry and she decided to study. Jimena was the first in her family to go to college. She went to nursing school and soon met a nice school teacher. They waited almost ten years to have Sophia. Everyone loved Sophia because she was easy-going and sweet. She was an elementary school teacher and now she is marrying an accountant. The couple looked like the Latin version of Ken and Barbie. They looked simply stunning and the wedding was beautiful. There was her cue and Sabina came out to sing **Ave Maria**, her gift to the couple. Sabina looked and sang her best.

The wedding went on without issue. Sabina was not sure if Steven was in the audience, but she did not really care. She stopped to throw some bird seed. Then she set her GPS to make her way to the reception hall. Sabina was happy she had some time to get lost since the wedding party was busy taking pictures. Sabina found a nice parking space and she decided to send a few pics to Bill while she waited. Still no response from him, 'don't overthink it, Bill must be traveling,' Sabina told herself.

She walked into the reception hall and looked for the wedding planner. Sabina told her that she had prepared one song and once it was over, she was planning to go home.

"I don't want any drama. My ex and his new girlfriend are here. I just want to sing and go. You think you can help me out?"Sabina pleaded with the wedding planner.

"Sure, if you want you can skip the wine and cheese reception. You can go inside and go upstairs for a bit. I will text you in a few minutes before you go on. No worries, you can sing and then go" the nervous lady said.

Sabina thought "Great, my parents must be smiling over me." Sabina then made her way to one of the rooms upstairs. She watched the cars pull in and park. She did not care that she was not mingling with them. Sabina was just enjoying the peaceful environment and waiting to hear from Bill. "What is going on with me? She thought, "I really like Bill and I am sure he likes me. I am going to go for it. I deserve to be happy. I am sure William will make me happy." She then started scrolling through her pictures and found one with them in the Rocky Mountains. Sabina was daydreaming when she was rudely interrupted by the wedding planner's text message.

Sabina came down the staircase and began singing **Marry Me** by Train. She knocked it out of the park and then some of the wedding party were dancing, people were on their feet and Sabina did feel like a rock star. But as she sang her last note she felt someone glaring at her. 'It's Steven' she thought. And when she looked over, her worst fears were confirmed; it was Steven and he was drinking. Sabina knew that she could not stay long. She ran upstairs, grabbed her wrap and purse and headed for the door.

Sabina made it downstairs to find the wedding planner waiting for her. "I need a favor please. Can you stay and sing a few more songs? The other singer has not arrived. The DJ is going to play the Chicken Dance and then nothing. Can you please stay for a few minutes?" Sabina agreed and handed over her wrap and purse.

"I will sing a few selections and then I am out of here." The dress Sabina was wearing was structured with strings that would show her legs. She was wearing the dress in a very conservative manner, but the wedding planner took it upon herself to show a little leg by hiking up one side of the dress. Sabina reluctantly agreed and she went on to the stage. She sang a few songs just to buy time for the band and the singer to arrive. Then Martina came up to the stage drunk and started heckling Sabina. She attempted to ignore her, but then Steven and his new girlfriend moved closer to the stage. Sabina got the signal that the musical group had arrived. She decided to sing **This Girl is on Fire** as the final song. She belted out the last lyric and ran off the stage.

Sabina grabbed her stuff and made her way to the parking lot. She was so excited to video chat with Bill. The call started to connect as she unlocked her car.

"Hello Sunshine, how was the wedding? You look amazing." Bill said.

"Hey you. How are your military inspections?" she asked with excitement.

"Look out Sabina!" Bill yelled out.

Sabina was struck from behind and when she managed to drop her wrap and purse inside of her car, the phone landed on the seat, but Bill could not make out what was happening.

"Who do you think you are, Bitch?" Steven said while he slapped Sabina in the face and tore off the strap of her dress. She could smell the alcohol coming from his breath. She pushed him off, knocking him on the ground.

"Stay away from me Steven. You are drunk." She tried to open the door when his new girlfriend, Cindy, pulled her by the hair.

Sabina widened her stance and pushed Cindy off of her.

"Handle your man Rookie." Sabina yelled as she watched Cindy on the ground.

"You stay away from me Steven and keep your dog on a leash" Sabina said while getting in her car.  As she tried to pull away she noticed Martina capturing the entire thing on her cellphone.

"We got you now Sabina. I am calling the cops and telling them you hit Steven. You are going to jail and you will lose your job" Martina yelled.

"I got you Bitch. I know you think you're all that. Puta, I saw you video-sexting with a guy. You are just another whore, you fat-ass pig" Steve yelled, "Call the cops Martina, this Bitch is headed to the slammer."

Sabina took a deep breath and sped home. She was distressed and hysterically crying, and she did not know where her cell phone was. All she wanted was to get home safely and get out of the ripped dress. Oh God, she thought, William, she needs to talk to him. What if he saw the whole thing? What must he be thinking? Holy crap! William! Sabina got to her driveway just to see that her porch light was out. Damn, she thought if the phone was dead, then she would never be able to find it. It is too dark for this, she thought. She ran inside and sent him an email. Sabina prayed that he would check his school email to see that she was okay.

Sabina decided she needed to get some rest. This day was too much. She sat on her bed and began to cry uncontrollably. In her mind, she lost William forever. She was so mad at herself. Why did she have to go to the wedding? She did not have anything to prove. She called out "William, William," and wondered why she was so stupid. She was falling in love with him. Why was she sabotaging a good relationship? She felt damaged and used and now to add insult to injury Steven was going to take her job.  Sabina was just inconsolable and fell asleep from the exhaustion.

Sabina was awakened by someone pounding at her front door. She grabbed her shotgun and went to confront the intruder. She racked the chamber as she approached the front door. Sabina told herself, 'No matter who is on the other side of this door I will survive.' "What do you want? It is 1:00 AM. Anyone standing on the other side of this door better get ready to meet their maker. I mean it!! You better get with Jesus before I introduce you."

She stood near the door ready to shoot when she heard, "Sunshine it's me, William, Bill. I am ready for a lot of things but let me check on you first before I meet Jesus."

Sabina placed the shotgun behind the door and opened the door to see Bill standing there. She melted into his arms and collapsed. She was so confused and grateful to him for being there at this moment. He pressed himself against her body and held her tight. It was more than an embrace; it was as if their souls were connecting at a cosmic level. Finally, after several minutes, Bill took a step back and said,

"What can I do to make it better for you?"

"Nothing, it's a huge mess. My life is a mess and I am messy. I cannot believe you are here. How are you here?" Sabina said.

"Let's go inside and I will get you some tea while you change and clean yourself up" Bill responded, leading her inside.

Sabina looked at herself and began to cry more,

"Oh Lord, I'm a mess. Why would you want to be involved with this?" she protested.

"Don't be mean to my friend Sunshine. You are an amazing woman going through a battle. Only a coward would strike when your back is turned. I saw that coward and I wanted to punch him in the face. That is his issue not yours. You are strong, beautiful, and you are my friend. I don't have many friends so the few I have I guard with my life" Bill said.

Sabina took a deep breath and looked at her formerly beautiful dress. The strap was ripped and the material was stretched. Her left breast was almost exposed and she had scratch marks and bruises near her neckline.

"Go take a nice hot shower and I will work on your tea. Where is the kitchen?" Bill said. Sabina pointed and then told him,

"Thank you. I will pull myself together and go upstairs to shower" Bill nodded and walked to the back of the house.

Sabina took off the dress and flung it on a chair. She started the shower and waited a few minutes for the steam to envelop the entire bathroom. As she stepped into the warm water she could still smell Steven's alcoholic breath near her face. Sabina began reliving her latest nightmare with him. She began to shiver and cry. Despite the warm water, her body was frozen and she could not move. The water was turning colder now and she knew she had to get out of the shower, but she simply couldn't. She closed her eyes and whispered, "William, William." Like magic he appeared,

"Come on Sunshine, let's get you out of there." Bill stood with a towel ready to wrap her up and warm her.

"I got your tea and I pulled down the covers for you. I don't know what you wear for pajamas, but I like to be comfortable. I hope you don't mind wearing one of my T-shirts." He lifted her arms and dressed her with a tan shirt that read "US Army."

"Whenever you are ready, release that wet towel and I will hang that up for you" Bill instructed.

Sabina dropped the towel as if she were dreaming. He then helped her sit on the edge of the bed and laid her underneath her covers.

"Let me look at those marks," Bill inquired. "They don't look too bad. I will grab you some ice and that should help. Did you drink anything tonight? No?" Bill asked. "I will run downstairs and get you some Motrin. It will help with the swelling. Just close your eyes and I will be right back. I promise I'm not going anywhere" Bill scooted out of the room. Sabina's head was spinning; she could not control her emotions; she was having a full-blown panic attack. Her body began to shake again and the room was still spinning.

Bill walked in and noticed that she was clutching her pillow for dear life. He immediately jumped into action.

"I got you. I am here. You are not alone. I am here. You are going to be okay. You are having a combat episode aka a panic attack. I need you to open your eyes and look at me. Then breathe we will get through this together. I am here. I got you. Breathe for me" Bill told her as he laid next to her. Bill could feel Sabina's body responding to him. She was no longer shivering and she managed to control her breaths.

"Here, sip some water and take the Motrin. Are you feeling a little better?" Bill said in a very compassionate tone.

"I am more embarrassed than ever, Bill. I don't know what came over me. I don't have panic attacks" Sabina said.

"You probably do and just don't know it. When humans face great dangers day in and day out they become accustomed to the adrenaline dump. We compartmentalize fear and store it until one day our brains have an overload. Normally we have panic attacks while we are sleeping and we just call them nightmares. Sometimes our bodies can't wait for us to be asleep and it has to push it all out through a panic attack. Clearly they are trigger-based and I am not a shrink but I think your Ex is your trigger."

"Bill, I don't know what to do. He has got me by the short hairs. My family loves him and they keep inviting him to our events. I cannot get away from him. He is a detective at the local police department and has strong connections with my Sheriff. I cannot believe things got so out of hand. I still don't know how you got here. Why are you here?" Sabina demanded to know.

Bill pulled himself closer to Sabina. He wanted her to know no matter how hard she fought him off he was going to be with her.

"I was trying to tell you earlier that I was heading to Florida, but I did not get a chance. I landed at MacDill Air Force Base and then traveled to a place called Apopka, Florida. I got your address when you ordered your dress. I thought I could surprise you. When I saw that asswipe strike you, I told my crew I had a family emergency and they went ahead without me. It's all good, they are inspecting a few small stops and heading back home. So, I can be here as long as you need me" Bill responded.

"Bill, my life is complicated, you just don't understand. I am helpless with this. I cannot report Steven, he has all the power" Sabina said.

"You think this doesn't happen in the military? It takes place daily. Some asshole thinks that just because he is in the Army, the Navy or the Marines, that he can beat up a female soldier. My little sister, Ellis, well, she is like my sister, joined the Marines. Tough right? She met some jerk who promised her the world. I found out that he was taking out his shortcomings on her face. So, my buddy Scott and I tried to hunt him down. Ellis, Ellie, was forced to work with the system and make a report. That asshole got bounced off the base and arrested before we got there.  I can assure you the United States Military does not stand for domestic abuse and neither should your agency. Let me help you."

"Bill, as a female officer, I cannot go and get a restraining order on my ex-husband who is also a policeman. It is not because he would lose his job. I don't care about his job, I am worried about mine. How can I ask guys to walk through doors with me if I can't stop my husband from hurting me? Do I need a piece of paper? What will a piece of paper do for me?"

"It is up to you and I will be with you no matter what you decide. However, I'm surprised at you. You are a peace officer and you deal with domestic violence all the time. You always tell victims to fight when they are ready. I know it's hard; you might not be ready to fight but I will fight with you, " Bill said.

Sabina felt like a fool. She knew Bill was right, but she could not wrap her head around it. It was just too much for her. She was grateful Bill was there with her.

"I am just worried about my career. I know it is selfish and it's not what I should be focused on, but since my parents died, it is all I have" Sabina said.

"What happened to your parents if I may ask? " Bill asked.

"My father immigrated to Miami from Cuba. He came to America with $30.00 in his pocket. He worked really hard until he saved enough money to put a down payment on a bakery. Soon he opened Contreras Conchitas Bakery and he paid for his brother to join him in Hialeah. The bakery was successful and soon my Dad was happy and he reached his American Dream. He met my Mom at church and they were married not long after. My parents were good, respectful, church-going people. When the hurricane hit south of Miami, my parents went to help. My Dad baked bread, made Cuban sandwiches, and loaded cases of water to hand out. When they were ready to leave my Mom and Dad came over to tell me they were heading out. I told them I would go with them if they waited one more day. My agency was sending people down there so they could follow us. My parents did not want to wait. They said people were in need. They were missionaries and Jesus would protect them. I guess Jesus was busy that day. I was told they drowned when they took a wrong turn and ended up on a bridge that was wiped out by the flood waters. Amazing isn't it? My parents were doing the right thing but I guess Jesus fell asleep at the wheel."

"Jesus did not fall asleep at the wheel. It was just their time to move on. I am sorry for your loss" Bill said.

"I know my parents were doing the right thing, but I miss them. I wish they were here so I would not feel so alone. They have been gone for five years and it still feels like they just died. Steven took full advantage of the situation. He and my uncle decided they were in charge of the estate. My Uncle Paco took over the bakery and said he would divide the profits evenly and I've yet to see a dime. Steven must be taking it but I cannot seem to find out. After the divorce, I moved into this house. My father built it for my mother. It was her dream house and their dream to retire and move away from it all. They loved Polk County since it is right in the middle of the state. My mother supported my dream of becoming a police officer. My dad wanted me to be a teacher, but soon enough he was happy for me. Mom talked me into joining the Polk County Sheriff's Office. I met Steven in the academy; he was sponsored by Crystal Lake P.D. We fell fast and ours was a whirlwind romance and soon enough, we were married. Sometimes you marry the wrong person but you stay married because of ideals. Even when things are bad you stay because of loyalty. One day you wake up and you no longer recognize who you are anymore" Sabina said.

"You know, you don't have to tell me your story if you are not ready and don't want to. I am here either way" Bill said.

"It's okay like I said, sometimes we get stuck with the wrong person. Steven made sure I was isolated from everyone. When my parents were killed, the isolation was even worse. I was such a fool to think Steven would change, but he did not. The only one who was changing was me and I did not like who I was turning into. Steven started drinking more and more. He was drunk all the time even right before a shift. I don't know how he made detective, but he did. I think because he was in an office and not on the street. We had a house near highway 27, close enough for us both to get to work. I got home one day and Steven had never made it to work.

He had spent the entire day drinking. When I asked him what was going on, he just called me a bitch and

pushed me. We fought like a real hand-to-hand combat thing. Ultimately, he pinned me down and I was branded

with his cigar. Steven knocked me out and when I woke, he was gone. I packed what I could take and moved

into my parents' retirement home. I left Steven that day and filed for divorce. It wasn't too messy. I gave him

everything we had except for my parent's estate. He could not touch that. Not my parent's account, bakery, or

house. This became my safe haven and it has been for the past years" Sabina said.

Sabina could smell Bill's scent and her body was overcoming the grief. She did not want him to see her

vulnerable, but at this moment Sabina was happy Bill was with her. She no longer felt lost.

"I am just so mad, Bill. The whole thing was captured on Martina's cell phone and she put it on social

media. I am the laughing stock of my family, my community and my job" Sabina revealed.

"Or, you can pull yourself together when you are ready, and fight. They have given you enough

ammunition to hang them all. It is all up to you. What are you prepared to do? You are no longer alone. What if

it was not you but someone else you cared about in this situation? What advice would you give them? How do

you fight off a wolf or a pack of wolves?" Bill said in a soft tone of voice as he stroked her hair.

"I would tell them to save the video for evidence, apply for a restraining order, and walk tall." Sabina

replied with conviction. They went on to talk for several more hours, when they heard a car speed into the

driveway. Next they heard a door slam with a loud bang. Sabina began to shake a little and Bill could tell it was

not a friend who came to check on her.

"Steven is here. I guess he was not done with me. He must be really drunk. When he gets three sheets to

the wind, he stands outside and yells. I am the cause of all his troubles. Last time, I called his Supervisor and

they drove him home. I don't have my cell phone; it's in the car. I hate to have to go down to face him" Sabina

said as she rose.

"No you are not alone and my father raised more than a man, he raised a gentleman and a warrior. I got this. Just stay here. I promise not to kill him. But I can't promise much more than that" Bill said with a wicked smile.

Bill stepped out of the house and stood in the shadows while Steven was pacing back and forth yelling, screaming, and cursing. Steven was calling for Sabina to come out. Sabina decided to get dressed by putting on some joggers, a hoodie, and sneakers. She waited to hear from Bill so she could come out.

"Fuck you Bitch, come out and face the music. Come on out, you whore. Sophia told me you got a man. Is he satisfying you? Come on you Bitch, if you don't come out I will come in and get you. I will show you a real man. That is what you are missing, a real man" Steven yelled.

Bill stepped out of the shadows and got between Steven and the front door. Steven turned around and heard someone say,

"You need help or are you looking for someone?" Bill said in a mild tone.

"Step out of my way boy before you regret it" Steven said.

"Look Mister, I don't know who you are or what you want. But it's time for you to move on. So move on, Boy" Bill responded.

"Hey, I had about enough of you. This is a domestic issue between a husband and a wife. You don't have any business in our business. If I were you, I would walk away. Sabina is a whore and she ain't worth your time" Steven said.

"So I take it you're just a foul-mouthed piece of shit. You need to move on. You are not welcome here anymore" Bill said.

"Fuck you" Steven said while he took a step towards Bill.

Bill stood his ground and did not back off.

"I am not going to repeat myself. This is a simple thing: you go home and I will not be forced to hurt you" Bill said.

"Fuck you! I don't care if you are a soldier or not. I am a Cop and I can arrest you or kick your ass. Either way I am safe. You are in my house. So you and what Army is going to move me out of my wife's place?" Steven said.

"Ok, we will try this your way one time. I don't need my fellow soldiers to move you. Now you better get moving or do I need to kick your ass all the way up the road? The way I figure it's about ½ mile up the road and by the time I am done kicking your butt, I will be ready for a nice hot breakfast at the nearest IHOP" Bill said.

Steven pulled out a pocket knife and flung it out towards Bill. Bill jumped back and pulled off his belt then wrapped it around his fist.

"Come on Soldier, let's see what you got?" Steven stepped forward with the knife at Bill.

Bill wrapped the belt around Steven's wrist and quickly disarmed him. Then with one swift move Bill had Steven in a headlock. Sabina opened the door and yelled out,

"Bill, stop. Please don't get into trouble. Don't, please don't!" Sabina cried out.

"Sabina don't worry, I will not hurt him. I promise to just get into his car and drive it up to the street. I will walk this person to the street. He is in no condition to drive himself. I suggest you call your Supervisor to come out and get you" Bill said.

Sabina jumped into Steven's car and drove it towards the street. Sabina put his keys inside of the glove box. She stood outside and waited for Bill to come up from the house. The roadway was dark and Sabina did not grab her flashlight or cell phone. She was left to wait and pray for Bill not to kill him. Bill walked Steven up the road while still holding him tight around the neck until they got to the edge of the road.

"Now that you are off Sabina's property, why don't you call your boss to come get you? Or do I have to call the local P.D.? What is your pleasure? You call or I call?" Bill said.

"Fuck you! I am not calling anyone" Steven said.

Bill took out his phone while still holding Steven still with one arm.

"From my understanding this is Polk County jurisdiction and the wedding was in Polk county jurisdiction. You are Crystal Lake Police and since you work in the city your authority ends at the city limits" Bill said.

"Ok, I will call my Sergeant but he will arrest you. I swear he will throw you in jail for a long time" Steven yelled as he dialed from his cell phone. Bill released Steven and dropped him to the ground.

"Listen, if you get up I'll drop you as many times as it takes. You are drunk and I don't want to hurt you, but I will" Bill ordered.

"Fuck you Asshole. Hello, Serge, it's Steven Goodwin. I need you to come to Sabina's house. It's an emergency, there is a guy holding me while we wait for you to come and arrest his ass" Steven yelled into the cellphone.

Bill and Sabina waited for the Sergeant to arrive at Sabina's house. It was not long when they could hear tires speeding towards them. A black sedan pulled over near where Bill and Sabina stood, near Steven's car. The door opened and a tall white male stepped out with an angry look on his face. He was staring at Steven.

"Goodwin, what the fuck? I told you it was not a good idea to go to that stupid wedding. You are a drunken mess. "Get your ass in the car," the Sergeant barked his orders. Steven stood up and wobbled towards the car.

"Fuck the Army and fuck you too, whore." Steven yelled.

Bill took a step forward as he got ready just in case Steven got stupid and tried to attack him or worse, Sabina.

"What the fuck! Deputy Goodwin? Why is Detective Goodwin beaten up? You know what kind of trouble you have got yourself into with this little stunt?" the Sergeant yelled.

"Are you fucking joking Sergeant Dumb Ass? You got your officer here outside of the city jurisdiction punching on his ex-wife. He drove drunk in what appears to be a police officer- issued vehicle. Detective Steven Goodwin is currently intoxicated and breaching the peace. And you Sir have no authority here. I am about to call her boss. I hear he is a righteous kick-ass kind of guy who will be more than happy to display two pieces of shit on television" Bill said.

"You don't scare me, soldier. You call anyone you want, right Sergeant?  We are good. Let's kick his ass" Steven yelled while trying to get up from the ground.

"Shut the Fuck Up, Steve. You're the dumb ass now, you got us both in a jam. I told you to stay away from her. You don't have any business here. Hell, I ain't got no business here either. Get your ass into my truck. I will drive you home. Where are the keys to Steve's car? If you give them to me we will get out of your hair" the Sergeant said.

"Inside of the glove box," Sabina said.

"Look Goodwin, I don't really know what all took place tonight. I am not sure how much trouble you want Steve to get into. I came just as a courtesy to pick him up and get him out of your hair. If you feel like in any way he offended you or mistreated you there are avenues set up for this type of thing. I would ask you to take it seriously since it might cost Steve, a good cop, his badge. And you might get damaged as well. So think long and hard before you call Internal Affairs" the Sergeant cautioned Sabina.

"You piece of shit. You guys are all alike; this shit happens in the military all the time. You think because she is a woman she should take this abuse. Yes Sir, abuse. First you allow your officer to do what he wants with no consequences. Then you threaten her and when that does not work you get scared for your job and make her feel bad. You have got to be kidding me. If you don't get out of here, I will be more than glad to kick both your asses" Bill said.

"I know what I need to do and I don't need to be lectured by anyone. You take your man and make sure he does not come back to my house. I will be seeking a restraining order and if he does not comply I will have him arrested. And yes, I will be reporting this incident to my agency with full disclosure" Sabina said with conviction.

The Sergeant pushed Steven into his truck and drove off. Sabina and Bill looked at one another.

"You want to wait a few minutes to see if they come back for the car or do you feel like hoofing it back to your place?" Bill asked.

"Bill, I don't care when they come back for the car. Let's just walk back and try to get some rest" Sabina replied.

They walked together to the house in silence. Bill did not want to push the issue with Sabina, he understood she was stuck in a position.

"Who takes care of your animals? Do you need me to feed them in the morning?" Bill asked.

"Oh, no Bill, you don't have to worry about them. The Garcias, my neighbors, Juan and Este, will come by in the morning. I pay them to handle their care. They will come by in the morning and move the animals from one field to the next and clean the barn. To be honest, I am too tired to think about it tonight. I don't know about you, but I am exhausted" Sabina said.

"I am pretty beat, too," Bill said.

"I can fix you a room in the house tomorrow. Do you mind just crashing with me tonight? "We are both pretty tired. Are you good with that?" Sabina said.

"I am good at crashing anywhere. If you like, I can sleep on the couch or by the door. I can drop anywhere, honestly"

They walked into the house and to the kitchen. Once there Sabina looked at Bill and noticed his shirt was ripped and cut. Bill was bleeding from the cut.

"Oh God, that asswipe must have gotten me with his knife" Bill said, "You got a place where I can go and clean up" Bill asked.

"I am so sorry Bill. Just go upstairs into my bathroom and you can clean up there. If you want you can take a shower and there are band-aids and a first aid kit. Make yourself at home. There are clean towels in the cabinet" Sabina said as she was falling asleep on her feet.

"Okay, let's make a deal; we will both go upstairs and you can rest while I can take that nice hot shower" Bill said.

Bill grabbed his 'go bag' and he walked upstairs with Sabina. Sabina decided to change into something more comfortable. She picked her oversize man's shirt nightgown. She was too tired to look for anything else and then slipped into her bed while Bill went into the bathroom. He took off his t-shirt and found one small cut above his abdomen. He found the first aid kit and he got the shower going. Bill wanted to clean himself up and to get some shut-eye.

Sabina could see the steam seeping into her bedroom when suddenly Bill stepped out from the bathroom into the bedroom wearing only his unbuckled jeans. She tried so hard not to stare at him, but Sabina could not help it. Bill was a handsome man, but you could tell life had beat him into shape. Her attention was focused on his muscular chest. She saw the scars that were branded over his heart and just at the edge, a burn mark. Sabina wondered what the real story behind this man was. As Sabina glared she could see the ruggedness in Bill's stature. He was the tall and muscular type, rough and tough in the right areas. Bill took another step and caught her looking at him and he smiled at her. She couldn't help it. He was wearing jeans and nothing else.

"You sure I can sleep here with you?" Bill asked.

"Yes, I promise to keep my hands to myself," Sabina said, embarrassed.

"Well I promised nothing, but I will not take advantage of the situation. Tonight we sleep" Bill responded. While he slipped into the bed and pulled his body next to Sabina's, he could feel her tension and the exhaustion emitting from her body. He held her tightly with one arm around her waist while softly stroking her hair. Bill loved the way her skin felt next to his bare chest. Her perfume invaded all of his senses and drove him crazy. However, he needed to focus on her and take care of her tonight. He wanted to make sure Sabina felt safe and secure but he could not help thinking about them together. He enjoyed her company so much he never wanted moments like this to come to an end. Bill could sense with every minute Sabina was letting her guard down and he was winning her over. Bill was confident that Sabina was the right person for him, but he did not want to scare her away. He knew she was hesitant, traumatized, and frightened. Bill thought 'in the morning light we'll figure it all out.'

"Close your eyes Sunshine I got you. You are not alone. I am here. I will always be here for you. I got you, it's ok." Soon both Bill and Sabina were asleep.

# 7

## The Morning After

BILL WOKE UP with the first light. He felt refreshed and content as he slipped gently and quietly out of Sabina's bed. He made sure not to wake her as he made his way downstairs in order to search for coffee. "Boy" he thought "She is Latina. I'm going to find the strong stuff here." He opened one or two cabinets to find good old-fashioned coffee. He brewed them two cups and took a tray upstairs. Bill placed Sabina's cup next to her bed on her nightstand as he slipped back into bed with her. The strong aroma woke her up and he whispered "Good Morning" as she reached for the coffee.

"Hello" she said "What are you doing in my bed?" Sabina said as she took a sip of coffee.

"You don't remember?" Bill said with a confused look on his face. Sabina began to laugh wickedly.

"You are kidding me? You set me up? Really? Give me that coffee Lady, you don't deserve it" Bill said.

"Oh come on, it was a little funny. You should have seen your face. Thank you for the coffee. I really needed it" Sabina said.

"You deserve a whole lot more, but all I could find was coffee" Bill said while sitting up in bed. "You feeling better?" he asked.

"I can't recall the last time I slept this good. It was amazing, thank you. How about you? I guess I am not a good hostess. Give me a minute and I will finish this and I will get your room ready if you like" Sabina said in a hurry.

"Stop, I am good. I had a good night. You relax for a minute. Come on" Bill opened his arms and signaled Sabina to lay her head on his chest.

"I am sorry it has been a long time since I was with a man. I guess I don't know how to act" Sabina explained.

"You are fine. I enjoy everything about you, even your insecurities. Really just enjoy your coffee and the moment of peace. I know I am. Unless this is too much and you need me to back off" Bill said.

"No, I just need you to be here and I need to be here. This is really nice" Sabina said as she placed her cup on Bill's side on the nightstand. She accidentally tapped her sound system and light music started playing in the background. Her hand then brushed over Bill's chest and she lightly rubbed the rough skin which had been scarred. He took her hand and held it there for a second.

"You want to know what happened there. You want to hear the story of my life and how I got damaged?" Bill said.

"I am curious I will not lie to you, but it's your story to tell whenever you are ready" Sabina responded.

"Sabina, I can tell you anything I promise not to have secrets from you not today or ever. If you want to know the story of my heart I will share it with you" Bill said in a very serious tone. Sabina stopped rubbing his chest and left her hand over his scars. Bill sat his cup next to hers and began telling her,

"I was married for a long time to Patricia. As far back as I can recall, she was in my life. We were inseparable and I thought life was going the way it should be going. We had our careers and a nice home after being married for 14 years. I really believe she was all I needed. I thought we were happy. Or at least that I made her happy. That is what you tell yourself when you give up who you are to make someone love you right? I gave up who I was and gave in all the time. Truthfully, she broke my heart and it shattered like a rock through a cheap window. I never saw it coming. So much for military Intel training.

My wife was so cold, her indifference cut me like a knife and she took my soul. When she left, which now I know was the best thing that could happen, I was lost. I could not tell people how or why she left because I still don't know. It made me question everything and put my love on ice. Patricia, Pat left me for another man and moved away. I was humiliated at the base. The great Ghost got ghosted by his old lady. I know that is ego, but it was more than pride. It was a heartache and I needed to get it out. I know it sounds dramatic and maybe even pathetic but a person will do crazy stuff when they are hurting. And believe me, I was beyond mourning the end of the marriage. I was in agony. It hurt so much, I thought that I would just cut my heart out. Like a drunken fool I did; I grabbed my army knife and started to cut and cut until that pain woke up all my senses.

I was a fool to give up so much of myself to a woman who did not appreciate it. That pain slapped me back into life. Pain is a way to let your body know that it is still alive. I was alive, damaged and wounded, but alive. I had an honest conversation with myself. I was very unkind to the idiot that faced me in the mirror, but I needed it. I got up even though I wanted to stay down and called the one person who has always been by my side. I called my Dad and told him I needed to come home. I needed the clear blue sky, and to feel the motherland on my fingers. I need to be with my father. He said, 'I've been waiting for you. Come home.' In a blink of an eye, I found myself in Wyoming looking at the vastness of the land and taking a real breath for the first time.

My dad saw my scars and he told me he had a vision that I was coming home. He helped me pull myself from the bottom up and we worked the ranch. One day Pop told me, "the older you get the better you will feel. You know you only live for a minute, better enjoy it while you're in it, because it's gone in a blink. Get out of here and go find your destiny. Your love is out there. Go son, get started, life is short, your spirit needs his companion." "I love my dad, but that day I thought he was just saying his old Sioux tribe tales. What did he know about my spirit and my pain? One night he took me for a vision quest at the top of the crest. It is a sweat lodge that lasted about five hours. The ceremony had four rounds at about 120 degrees. By the time you are on your third round, you are either cleansed or hallucinating. I was somewhere in between when the vision came to me. I needed to do something more and break away from my pattern to clear the way to my heart" Bill stopped for a minute and then continued

"I know this is a lot, but I know what I want and who I want and how to love. I am ready and I can wait for you forever if you are not. I know you are my companion. My soul cries when you are not near me. Sunshine, I know you are the one who is supposed to be in my path."

Eric Clapton's song **If I Could Change the World** was playing in the background and Sabina found herself hypnotized by Bill's story.

Sabina could not contain herself and she placed her lips over his mouth and whispered, "William, William" and gave herself to him. Sabina wanted this moment to last an eternity. She felt safe and warm as his fingers intertwined with hers and the sensual feeling deep down in her body was one she never experienced before. As he pulled her closer to him she became drunk with passion as his scent, what's that scent? It was like a force field she could not resist. She had the urge to kiss his neck. Bill slightly moaned which made her wetter. He caressed her shoulders and moved his arms down her back and slowly unhinged her bra. He kneeled down to kiss her abdomen and slowly unbuttoned her shirt. Bill was imagining this scene for the last few days. Her breasts were beautiful, and now they are his. He moved up to kiss her breasts. Sabina let out a moan and she moved her hands through his hair. She wanted him there and yet she wanted him everywhere else.

When they kissed, it was forceful and she wanted more. She slid down his pants and looked at his erection. She held it and wanted it much closer to her body. Bill was pleased and slid her panties off and slowly moved her up the bed. He kissed her mouth and neck and then moved all the way down until he was in the cradle of her womanhood. The sensation and rhythm of his movements and his mouth quickly made her come. No, she has never before had an orgasm like this. Bill's erection needed to find its home and he kissed her before she could even catch her breath. Sabina wanted Bill inside her and as she wrapped her legs around his scarred and beautiful body he entered her and never wanted to leave. Their lovemaking was no match for anything they ever experienced before this moment and they climaxed together with the intensity equaling their growing love.

As the morning light broke through the window, Bill found himself kissing Sabina's forehead. It was close to daybreak, around five or so, and he watched Sabina for a while sleeping. A feeling of fear came over him and he began thinking Sabina was going to wake up and ask him to leave. Bill shook off the devil on his shoulder who kept whispering in his ear. He knew they were doing the right thing and it felt so right. He gave in to the idea they had done nothing wrong and Bill quickly fell back asleep. Bill hadn't slept like this in years. Bill held Sabina tightly next to him and began to dream. Sabina woke up to see Bill dreaming peacefully. He looked content and at peace. Sabina knew he was the right person to be with her at this moment.

She could not believe her own happiness, and the joy that he brought to her soul. They really connected at a level that could only be imagined by few. Sabina wanted him again, but she knew they needed to rest and recover. Sabina decided to slip away and go get them some food and sustenance. She brought a tray of coffee and pastries upstairs. Sabina did not want to wake Bill, so she set up their food on the balcony and she sipped her coffee while the sunlight began to shine over her pasture. As Sabina sipped her coffee, she peeked at Bill who woke up and made his way to her.

"Morning, Sunshine, did you sleep well?" Bill said.

"You know I did," Sabina said.

"Sunshine, is that coffee? Can I have some?" Bill asked.

"Of course, I got some pastries in case you got a sweet tooth," Sabina said in a coy manner.

"Man, I could smash some pastries right now," Bill said with a huge smile.

Bill and Sabina watched the sunrise together and recovered from their night of passion. Bill was done with his breakfast when he walked to the edge of the balcony.

"Sunshine, how big is your property? You want to show it to me?" Bill asked.

"Sure we can jump on the side-by-side and take a tour. I can be ready in a few minutes" Sabina said.

Bill ran to his truck to get himself a change of clothes from his 'go bag'. When he went back upstairs Bill could hear the shower going. He did not want to bother her so he decided to clear the dishes and wait his turn. Sabina stepped out of the shower and got herself dressed without missing a beat. She walked downstairs and made her way into the kitchen and found Bill washing the dishes.

"Hey what are you doing?" Sabina asked Bill.

"I was waiting for my turn to hit the shower. I guess that I can use the one down here after I finish cleaning things up" Bill said.

Sabina showed him one of the back rooms and Bill walked in to clean up. He lightly brushed against her but Bill did not push the issue. He walked into the room and dropped the bag onto the bed. Bill then went and took his shower, got dressed and looked forward to spending time with Sabina. Bill was ready in a matter of minutes due to his military training. He walked back into the kitchen and found Sabina putting on her a pair of boots that have seen better days.

"You ready?" Sabina said.

"Yep, I am good to go" Bill responded as he held the door open for Sabina. Sabina led the way to the shed behind her house. She jumped on the side-by-side and drove towards Bill, who was ready to jump in. They took off and headed towards the back of the property. Sabina was enjoying telling Bill about all she had learned being a "ranchera." She loved that her father wanted to give her mother a traditional Cuban life after they had retired from the bakery. Sabina told Bill all about her mother's love for animals and how her mother grew up in the rural side of Cuba. Bill enjoyed every second he spent listening to Sabina, who was a true storyteller. He wanted to capture her sense and her love for Mother Earth. They spent the day wondering and catching up and carrying on like children.  Bill could not recall the last time he has laughed so much. He felt like he was truly blessed to have found Sabina, his little ray of Sunshine.

"We better head in soon as the sun is about to set, but first I wanted to show you my garden. You still good?" Sabina asked as she was steering towards the barn.  The area was surrounded by barbed wire and fencing. It was very green with lots of different plants and vegetables. It appeared that Sabina had spent good money adding an independent irrigation system to ensure the quality of her product. As Bill walked around he could see that the ground was well kept and cared for. He was amazed by the type of dedication given to the garden.

"Sunshine, you really have a green thumb. This is amazing. What do you all grow down here in Florida? Bill asked.

"Since Florida is tropical, I have tried a few native fruits to see how they make out. I got papaya, avocado, and plantains over here. This area is more Americanized with strawberries, blueberries, and blackberries. I'm trying watermelon over there and guava here. I know each crop is different and requires their own care. My mother was very passionate about gardening and she taught me all I know. My dad built the fence and I recently had to put barbed wire to keep the deer out. They have been killing all my crops and I have tried everything to keep them out" Sabina said as Bill walked around sampling everything that was blooming. He looked like a little kid inside of a candy store.

"You tried putting human hair around the area? Deer are often scared of people so if they smell the hair it might keep them out" Bill suggested as he walked to the edge of the garden. He wandered into the jalapenos that were growing in pots near the fence. Sabina turned to see him placing a habanero pepper inside of his mouth.

"Oh God I hope you like hot stuff. Don't bite into it. Please don't.  Those are a crossbreed between habanero and ghost peppers. They came from the University of Florida; they are not for human consumption. Spit it out William!" Sabina ordered.

Bill started to laugh and with a mouth full of peppers he started to say,
"I am good. I love Indian food, Thai, and…Holy Shit! My mouth is numb!" Bill's face turned bright red and started to sweat profusely. He felt like he could not catch his breath and tears began rolling down his face.

"What the fuck?" he said as he was trying not to panic or pass out.
Sabina began to laugh as she walked him to the water barrel. Bill dunked his face into the water and stayed under the water as long as he could.  When he came up for air his face was finally returning to his normal tan color.

"You should stay out of the kitchen if you can't handle the heat, Soldier," Sabina teased him.

"You need to send those peppers overseas that shit will knock our enemy down and pray for death. What the hell is that? I can barely feel my face" Bill managed to say before going back into the barrel of water.

Sabina was trying not to laugh because she knew Bill was in pain, but she could not help herself. She rubbed on his back and comforted him. When she looked up she noticed the blue sky had turned towards another Florida thunderstorm. The sky was cloudy and she could spot lightning heading their way.

"Come on Bill. We need to find shelter. Let's go into the barn. There is a loft there with a shower on the second floor. You can take a nice cool shower and cool your body down. Don't worry the burning will stop soon enough.  Come on, lightning in this area is very unpredictable. You already got burnt once. Come on, I will help you inside" Sabina said as she led him into the barn.

"The loft is upstairs. Trust me it's pretty nice. I wanted to hire someone to live here or I even thought I would move in here while my parents were alive. It's more like an apartment that someone could share with the animals. I never did find anyone, but to be honest I never even looked."

Bill looked around and could see the enormous space with haystacks, and stools. Sabina held him up near the wrap-around staircase and they slowly made their way to the upper level.

They walked into what seemed like a home decor showroom; it was a beautiful space. The living room had a large couch and loveseat. There was a television, a small desk area, and a bookcase.  Bill could see the kitchen which appeared to be fully stocked, when Sabina turned his attention to the bedroom. Bill felt weak and almost like he was hung over so he leaned on her. Sabina had him sit on the bed while she turned on the shower.  Bill dropped onto the bed like a bag of rocks; he could not stand or catch his breath. When Sabina heard him gasping for air she ran towards him with a wet towel.

"William, William it's okay just breathe. In and out. It will pass in a few minutes. William I got you. Stay with me" Sabina said gently as she applied the wet cloth to his forehead. It took several minutes for Bill to regain consciousness and he finally managed to stop moaning from the pain.

"Are you alright? Do you think you can sit up?" Sabina said and helped Bill sit up enough to start taking off his shirt.

"Let's get you into the cool water. I am so sorry Bill, I did not think this would hit you so hard." Sabina said as she undid his pants and pulled them off. Bill was left with just his boxers as he tried to stand up. He was forced to hold on to Sabina while she carried him into the shower. They stepped underneath the water together as Bill allowed the water to rinse off his eyes and flush his body. The cold water was clearing his pours and he could finally see and no longer struggled to catch his breath.

"Oh Lord Sunshine, you can kill someone with those things. Wow, I feel like such a fool. You must think I am a wimp. But shit that hurts! I felt it down into my soul" Bill said while still holding Sabina. Sabina looked at Bill and smiled tenderly at him.

"You good?" Sabina asked while trying to pull away from him.

"Sunshine, I am good with you. Where are you going? "Bill said

"I thought you might not need me anymore," she said.

"Sunshine I will always need you and want you around. Come here I will show you what I mean." Bill said with that half-smile, half-smirk.

"I thought you were in too much pain," Sabina teased back.

"Sunshine on my deathbed, I would still want you. I would never turn you down. Come here let me show you" Bill stepped closer to her and kissed her. Sabina could feel every part of her body yearning for him. She could not help wanting him, but felt her insecurities and hesitation taking over. Sabina opened her eyes and saw that Bill had closed his while he reached to pull her into his space. She told herself that even if this was a fling she had to be present in the moment and she allowed herself to fall into Bill without reservations.

Sabina touched his chest and kissed him on his scar which made Bill quite aroused. Sabina's hands slid down his back and while Bill kissed her neck. He wanted them to be this way forever. Sabina didn't know what was happening to her but it was the happiest she has been in a very long time. She was falling in love with him. Bill wanted to kiss her lips but her lips had other plans and so she knelt down and looked at his engorged penis and started to pleasure him. He moaned so loud that Sabina thought he may still be in pain from the hot peppers, so she came up for air.

At this moment, Bill stroked her face and licked her lips and turned the shower off.  He took a towel and led her to the bed. She pushed his body to lay down then straddled her legs around his groin and they became one. Their bodies rocked and their moans grew louder and louder until the moment of climax. After, Sabina kissed him gently on his lips and on both his cheeks, her hair gently falling on his face and neck. "William, William." He loved when she said his name. "Sabina, you are amazing, I love you" Sabina paused, looking at him with that same love in her heart.


Sabina woke up finding herself in Bill's arms. He was not sleeping but rather caressing and kissing her. She did not want to wake up and held on as long as she could before saying,

"When do you have to return to the world?"

"I've got to leave tonight to fly back to Colorado."

Sabina got quiet and her thoughts began to consume her. Bill noticed her response and began brushing her hair with his hand.

"Listen Sunshine, I am the real thing. I need you to believe me. Once I fall for someone, I am devoted till the end. I know you are the one for me. I am not sure if you are there with me and I am willing to wait as long as it takes. But I need you to get into your thick hard head that you are it for me. So don't fall backwards, fall for me. I am a really good guy. I will not pressure you, but am begging you to give us a chance. This is too good to just be a fling. Alright? Please trust me" Bill said.

Sabina could not imagine seeing Bill off. She wanted to tell him how she felt, but she held off because she did not want to fall apart in front of him.

"I guess we should get up and figure out how to get you home," Sabina said.

"How to get me to base? Not home. My home is with you if you will have me, but I will not pressure you." Bill said as he stood up and put his jeans on and walked into the other room. Sabina laid in bed for a few minutes and then began the long task of dressing.

"Where are you heading? Colorado? Or do you have to stop in Atlanta first?" she said. While she made her way to Bill, he was looking at his cellphone. Bill looked up, his face was serious and he seemed distracted.

"Sunshine, it looks like things are progressing in the Sandbox. I might not be able to finish the leadership course. I am going straight back to my ranch and get things ready just in case. I don't want you to worry. Ok promise me you will think about what I told you about our future" Bill said.

"It looks like I need to drive to Tampa and fly straight to Colorado Springs. I am on standby for the next round of deployments. We will be together in a few weeks."

"You will be canceling the class in Washington then?" Sabina asked while looking out of the window and holding back her tears.

"Nope, I will make that one," Bill said, walking behind her and hugging her. "You will not get rid of me that easily. I might not make it to the last session, but we will be together soon. Besides, I promised to show you D.C when the cherry blossoms are blooming." Bill held on for a few minutes. He could feel her sadness and pain coming through her body heat. Bill did not want to make things feel worse for Sabina, and he decided not to tell her about his new mission.

"You want a ride to Tampa? I don't mind taking you" Sabina offered with a halfhearted smile.

"Well I got to take my buddy's car back to his station on Apalachicola" Bill responded.

"Apopka" Sabina corrected him, "I can follow you and then we can drive together to MacDill Air Force Base."

"You're the boss, Sunshine," Bill said as he grabbed his gear.

The ride was uneventful to drop off the car. Bill listened to some music, heard a few voicemails, and called his father.

"Hey Pops, how you doing?" Bill asked.

"Billy, your soul sounds at peace. Did you find your vision?" his Dad said.

"Hey Dad, you were right. I am so sorry I ever doubted you. I found her. My vision, my mission, my future wife, my true soulmate. I cannot wait to bring her home so you can meet her" Bill said.

"You found your Sunshine and that warms my heart, Son. I am at peace for you and I feel the spirit of your mother is content."

"Pops" Bill struggled to get the words out, "Mama would be pleased. I wish she was alive to meet her. Mama would fall in love just like I did with Sabina. I miss Mama a lot. I wish" Bill could not say more when his father cut him off

"Billy, your Mama knows you are happy. Just look out at the sky and see her smiling through the clouds. I am happy for you. It is about time your spirit stops wondering and settles down with a good, strong woman."

"Pop I am heading home and then back to the sandbox in a few weeks. I will tell you more when I land home. And Pop, I know I don't say it enough but I love you Dad" Bill said.

"You come home and I will prepare everything for you. Safe travels my son. Love you." And he hung up the phone.

Sabina pulled in behind Bill and quickly jumped into the passenger's seat.

"You alright? It looks like you were having a pretty intense conversation. Are you good?" Sabina asked.

"I called my Dad. I always call him when I am headed home. I guess it sounds cheesy but I always want him to know I am alive." Bill looked at Sabina who was trying hard to control her emotions. "Plus I wanted him to know that I met a crazy hot-tempered, hard-headed woman."

Sabina looked shocked at his words. Her facial expression was one of a hurt, and Bill wanted to make sure Sabina knew he was sure she was his girl but he took advantage of the situation. Bill could not contain his laughter. He had a laugh that could fill the room with joy.

"I told him that you were" Bill could not continue because he started laughing while Sabina started slapping his arm.

"No," Bill said, "I told him that you are amazing. I really want you two to meet. You would love my Dad and I am sure he will love you back" Bill said.

"Look Bill, we are going over the Sunshine Skyway Bridge. We are over the Gulf of Mexico. This is one of my favorite places in the world. The water is blue and clear and even though traffic is always thick, no matter where you are you can always see the water kissing the sky" Sabina said.

Bill looked outside and he could see the clear skies and it laid on top of the water as the waves were coming on the shore.

"We should not be far from the base, but do you want to stop for a few minutes?" Sabina asked.

"Absolutely. Can I see the water? I would love to put my feet in and walk in the sand with you even if it is just for a few minutes. Don't worry, they can't leave without me. So we have time. Not a lot of time but we got time" Bill said.

Sabina geared her car towards the exit and pulled into the beach parking lot. They pulled in and Bill immediately stepped out. As he looked over Sabina stripped off her shoes, socks, and rolled up her pants as she bolted towards the water. Bill tried to catch up but she had a head start and he did not catch her until she stopped. The strength of the waves knocked Sabina into Bill's arms.

"Amazing," Bill said.

"You like it? The view is breathtaking" Sabina said.

"That is not what is amazing. What is amazing is that you are always falling into my arms" Bill said as he held Sabina tightly towards him.

"You know that is not what I meant Bill," Sabina said.

"I know what I meant. You are amazing and I love the scenery as well" Bill said. "I want to kiss you and never stop kissing you. But I guess it's time for us to head out." Bill said
They kissed passionately for several minutes and Sabina pulled away "You better stop or I will not stop" Sabina said quickly.

Bill pulled her close one more time and kissed her.

"William, William," she whispered.

"Sunshine I know but I love it when you call my name."

Bill grabbed her hand and then lifted her into his arms and carried her back into the car. She drove him to base and Bill stepped out. Bill opened Sabina's door and pulled her out. He planted a great goodnight kiss on her. "You will wait for me. I will see you in D.C. in a few weeks and we will make up for lost time" Bill said.

"Yes we will see one another in Washington. Don't worry you don't have to room with Barb" Sabina said.

"I knew it, you are perfect for me." Bill said as he kissed her on the forehead and walked into the base. Bill turned to see Sabina's car pulling away.. He walked in and waited for his crew to take off. In a few hours he would be landing in Colorado Springs. Bill could still feel Sabina on him, from the scent of her perfume to her lips. He wanted to capture that feeling forever, but also realized that she was scared. Bill thought he better tread lightly not to spook her away. "I'm going to seek some wisdom from my Dad. He will tell me how to tame her fears." A few hours later Bill found himself driving to his ranch. He could not wait to speak to his father and get things settled for his new life.

**8**

# Life at the Ranch

BILL DROVE TO the edge of his ranch and at a distance he could see his father riding a horse. He was a strong rider and he and the horse appeared to be in perfect harmony and sync. Bill wondered if he could ever be as good of a tamer as his Pops.  He stepped back and held both his arms out embracing the land, wind, and sky. He was spotted by his father who quickly galloped towards him in a short-haired white and tan mustang.

"Welcome home Son. I could sense your happiness a mile away."

"Pops I am not sure how to describe what I am feeling but I am content" Bill responded.

"You are safe, you are home, you are happy. I am grateful to the spirits that guided you home."

"I am going to need your advice, Pops. I don't want to mess this up with her" Bill confessed. "I think I came on too strong and maybe she is not ready."

"Oh," his Dad smiled, "You come into the house and we will figure all your troubles out. I am pretty sure she is just like the wind in a hurricane just waiting to strike."

"Pop I am happy, but I am frightened as well. I have to go across the world and I don't want to lose her" Bill said.

"Come, come Son, life is short. Don't doubt the Spirits who blessed you with your soulmate. You think your mother did not come without work. I was in love with her and had to win her over.  Women are made to be two things beautiful and hot-headed. So come to the house we will sit and talk calmly." Bill got to stepping and made it to his home. Walking inside he could smell his father's famous homemade biscuits and gravy.

"You cooked?" Bill asked as his stomach was rumbling even more from the aroma.

"You were coming home and I knew you were in need of some good old-fashioned cooking. Not like your Mama's but close enough for comfort."

"Oh, Dad"

"I know this is going to be a hard deployment because now you got someone to come home to. Someone to worry about. Someone to miss. It would be easier if you just left and forgot about her, but you cannot. Your Spirit has tapped hers and now you are connected. You feel what she feels and soon enough once she opens her heart she will know all about you."

"Pops, how do I talk to her? I mean how do I tell her what is in my heart?" Bill asked.

"You are patient and kind to her. You take her as she comes lovely, sad, or broken. You are her other half even if she is shattered, you are together. If she is scared you are unwavering, and if she runs you stand still. It will be hard. It was the hardest thing I had to do. Your Mom was scared and filled with insecurities and I had to become her warrior. Once she stopped and realized I was with her forever she never left my side. Even today she rides alongside me. That is what I want for you. And the Spirits have made it happen so don't mess it up. Now you eat and rest, we will discuss it more in the morning" his father said as he walked out of the room.

Bill's mind would not stop racing. He had so many plans for Sabina and their future. He was not sure how they would do it if she was not willing to move to Wyoming or he had to relocate to Florida. He did not care which as long as they were together he thought. Bill had enough time in the service to retire if she did not want to move. With all the money he had saved throughout the years, they had more than enough to live comfortably anywhere. Bill thought if she wanted to they could do the snowbird thing and live in both places. He was just excited about the possibility of starting over. Bill said to himself 'I will do whatever it takes to make her happy. She is my mission and I hope to be hers.'

Each night Bill would either text or call his Sunshine. He always enjoyed listening to her day and telling her that everything would be alright. Sabina would share about some traffic stop or chase that she got into. She would tell him about some other officer who always sat underneath a tree and did nothing. They would laugh about something or other that happened on either side of the country. Bill would wait all day just to listen to her laughter. By the end of every conversation he would ask, "Sunshine, you still love me?" He would hear her silence and then she would whisper,

"You know I do."

Time just moved on without a hitch and both Bill and Sabina found themselves preparing for their trip to D.C.

"Bill, did you get a room? Or are you staying with me?" Sabina asked in an abrupt tone.

"I was going to ask you the same thing. I don't want you to feel obligated to stay, but I could really use the company. Your company specifically." Bill responded.

"I made the reservation before we got together. I hope you don't mind that it is not as nice as the last one" Sabina said.

"Well Sunshine I hope you don't mind. I called the hotel and I was added to the room. It's all paid for. You just need to grab a key once you get there. I will be landing around 1900 hours so I will catch up with you for dinner. Or sorry, do you want to have dinner with me? I didn't mean to assume" Bill said in a polite manner.

"Bill, you're a nut. Of course I will have dinner with you. I can wait for you and we can decide where to go or" Sabina said with a little giggle.

"Or we can order room service after we get reacquainted" Bill finished her sentence.

"You read my mind Bill. I miss you" Sabina added.

"Well Sunshine, do you still love me?" Bill asked.

"You know I do," Sabina whispered back.

"Good night Sunshine I will see you in a couple of hours at our nation's capital" Bill said.

9

# Cherry Blossoms in Bloom

BILL LANDED AT Reagan International Airport without incident. He made his way to the hotel and the convention center. He was excited to look for their room and see Sabina. Bill ran up the lobby and noticed all the people waiting for the elevator. He did not care that his room was on the eighth floor; he was bolting up the stairs to his girl. Bill walked in and found Sabina staring out of the window. Her heart skipped a few beats as she heard the door open. When Bill walked in, she was waiting for him with just a button-down shirt and barely anything else.

He dropped everything: his bag and keycard and ran towards her. He embraced her and held her body tightly. Bill brushed away her long curly hair and started kissing her neck.

He whispered, "Sunshine I missed you. I need you. I want you" Sabina reached behind and tried to pull his large frame towards her hips. She wanted him and their flaming passion was ignited. Bill could not contain himself and he kept searching for her skin. He needed to touch her and feel her heat. He braced her towards the window and kept kissing all over her curvy body. His mission tonight was to blow her mind.

"You were right, the cherry blossoms are spectacular," Sabina said in a nervous tone.

"You have no idea how beautiful you are, do you? I can't imagine being in this world in this room without being with you' Bill responded without hesitation. Bill had been thinking and lusting for her in his dreams, and this day this moment was finally here. They embraced with a passionate kiss. Her hands were groping his shoulders, chest, arms, back, and backside, His hands were in her hair, neck, down her back and butt. Bill saw her sexy panties and quickly removed them. Sabina began to unbutton his jeans. Bill fondled her breasts and kissed them. He brought her to the bed, where Sabina grabbed his hips. He entered her and she let out a loud moan which was only second to the one that Bill let out. Together they called out each other's names and climaxed quickly thereafter. It seemed that their passion for each other had no end. Bill wanted to ensure that Sabina was happy, as happy and satisfied as he was feeling. Bill went into the shower and when he came out Sabina was barely awakening. She opened her eyes to watch Bill pulling his jeans up. He had a hell of a body and she could not believe Bill loved her. She could feel herself falling for him and she was falling hard. Bill turned around and caught her peeking.

"I cannot believe you are here with me. Bill, you could be with anyone, why did you choose me?" she asked in a nervous tone.

"You are kidding. The only thing more beautiful than the blue sky is you, Sunshine" Bill said. She put her hands through his hair and he put his hand down her back and around her waist. Sabina felt so satisfied, but not quite as intense as the way she was feeling now that her hands were undoing his jeans and moving all the way down his skin where her fingers were wandering. His fingers also found her soft and smooth center. She let out a moan, and Bill asked if she was okay, but he knew she was." Oh William, I want you in me, next to me, on me."

William said two words, "I'm Yours."

Their hours of endless lovemaking found them famished..

"Hey Sunshine, you want to grab something to eat? " Bill asked.

"I am starving. I could eat. Do you want to eat here or go out?" Sabina said.

"I will leave it up to you. I am good either way" Bill said.

"Let's go for a walk and grab something anywhere," Sabina said.

Sabina got cleaned up and dressed. She threw on some jeans and a t-shirt with a thin sweater to cover herself up and tennis shoes. Sabina did not want to show off her body but in her attempt to cover herself up she looked gorgeous to Bill. Bill could not stop looking at her and thinking how grateful he was to have met her. They walked out hand in hand to search for food and refreshments. They were staying at the Gaylord Palms Hotel and the evening had brought out several people. The restaurants were booming with clients and the outside cafes seemed to be packed. As they walked near the boardwalk, they could see that there was no place to eat.

"You feel like hitting one of the food trucks and just sitting near the water?" Bill asked

"We can sample from a couple of places and try a little here and there maybe," Sabina said.

"I will grab a few things from the trucks over there and if you like, get us some drinks." Bill said.

They found a nice table and began to sample each one of the To-Go boxes. Everything seemed to be cooked perfectly. Bill and Sabina tasted everything. Sabina began to laugh out loud when she saw Bill had picked Mexican food which included jalapenos.

"You did not get enough at my place? Or are you looking for another cool bath?" Sabina said.

"Oh, God no, I cannot believe those things are in there. Keep them away from me. I will get nightmares and keep you up all night. I am not kidding, I am scared for my life. I told the guy I did not want them. He probably thought it was funny" Bill commented.

"Hey, let's walk that way. I can still hear the music playing and it looks like we are really close to the Ferris wheel." Bill said as he led Sabina towards the street party.

"Let's ride the Ferris wheel. Are you afraid, William? I'll take good care of you" Sabina took his hand and waited in line. She thought this was somehow a little too corny and felt a little more than embarrassed to be feeling this happy, this giddy, but really wanted to be close to him.

Bill reached over and kissed her hand and then gave her a huge kiss. "You taste wonderful. Look, we are at the top of the world and in a few seconds we could touch the sky." Bill tried to reach or pretend to reach it and the swing moved and Sabina grabbed onto the railing. Bill saw the fear in Sabina's eyes and he immediately said, "Oh baby I am so sorry. I was just playing around. I am so sorry baby, please forgive me." Bill began kissing her and holding her tight.

As they were ascending, their song comes on and Bill sings to her. "What is that song? I can't recall the name of it. What is the name of that song?" Sabina said.

**"I Can Dream About You"** Bill said all the while making sure she felt safe. As the seats lifted them and rocked gently into the air Bill softly began to sing to her the lyrics.

Bill sang "No more timing. Each tear that falls from my eyes I'm not hiding the remedy to cure this old heart of mine. I can dream about you If I can't hold you tonight. I can dream about you. You know how to hold me just right."

Sabina turned her full and undivided attention to Bill and soon enough they found themselves singing together. Sabina smiled and said, "You are not bad." She could not stop looking at his face, those beautiful eyes, those lips, and she kissed him.

"Sunshine, you know how I feel about you. You know you are in my heart?"

"William, William I am not sure if I am falling for you or if you already caught me" Sabina responded.

Sabina put her hands through his hair and his hands started to drift down her back as they found their way around her waist. Sabina felt overcome with passion, which quickly intensified when Bill's hands were undoing her jeans. He kissed her lips and neck and moved his fingers all the way down to her wet spot. She let out a few moans as she climaxed.

"Are you okay?" Bill asked even though he knew Sabina was just enjoying the moment.

"Oh, William, I want you in me, next to me, on me" Sabina managed to say again.

"I'm yours" Bill whispered as he continued to satisfy her.

Sabina and Bill managed to gather themselves together as they stepped off the Ferris Wheel and walked off the platform. They walked quietly for several minutes while looking for a more secluded area.

They stepped away from the public eye and found themselves all alone near the Potomac River.  They sat on a bench all to themselves. Sabina broke their silence by saying,

"I can't believe how beautiful and peaceful life seems up here. They sat on the bench and watched the calmness of the stream. Bill sat down and pulled Sabina into his lap holding her in his arms.  He wrapped himself around her and caressed her cheek. He exposed part of her neck and began kissing her gently. Sabina reached over and began playing with Bill's hair.

"This is perfect. I love spending time with you. I wish I could stop time for us. I know we are safe here and I don't ever want it to stop" Bill said.

Sabina leaned her body into Bill and she could feel a cell phone vibrating like crazy.  It was non-stop and it appeared to be urgent.

"You need to get that? It might be important" Sabina said.

"Not tonight. I don't want to get it yet. I want to stay here and I don't want to go back to reality. Not yet not tonight. Come on, stay here with me. Don't go anywhere not yet. Don't move, let me love you for a few more hours" Bill protested.

"We can stay a few more minutes but we will have to head in soon. We need to get up early and head into the seminar. You have to be at your best if you want to impress the group" Sabina said.

They were hit by a breeze and Sabina could feel a chill in the air. Bill could see that Sabina was cold and her light sweater was not enough to keep her warm. Sadly he felt it was time for them to go into their hotel. He stood up and pulled her up to her feet. They walked together while Bill attempted to keep Sabina warm. As they entered the hotel and made their way to their room. Sabina could see that something was bothering Bill. She could see that his cell phone was vibrating and he kept hitting the ignore button.

"Are you sure you don't want to answer that? It looks important" Sabina said.

"No, I will answer it in the morning. It will keep ringing but I am telling you it can wait till the morning" Bill said as he was unbuttoning his shirt.

"Are you ready for bed then?" Sabina asked.

"Yes I am beat. Let's hit the hay and try to get a few hours of shut-eye" Bill said.

They got into the big king-size bed. Sabina could not believe how tired she was and in a matter of minutes she began to fall asleep. Bill lifted her head onto his shoulder and laid her over his heart.

"Let's sleep. I got you and I am not going to let you go. Go ahead and close your eyes. I promise to wake you in the morning. Come on, don't fight your sleep. I got you, I will always keep you safe." She could not believe how kind and giving Bill was with her. She let go and finally fell asleep.

# 10

## Foolish Pride

AS THE MORNING sun shone into their room Sabina woke up to find Bill greeting room service at the doorway.

"What are you up to Bill?" Sabina questioned.

"I got you hot coffee and breakfast. You need it to fight off jet lag" Bill said as he brought over the food tray towards her. Bill's cell phone kept vibrating and lighting up.

Bill looked at it and mysteriously tried to cover it up. He reached for his cup of coffee and took a massive drink. His phone rang again and he could no longer ignore it. He looked at it once more.

"I have to take this call. I am sorry. I need to take this. Can I meet you downstairs? I am sorry." Bill said as he walked out of the room and into the hallway. Sabina was confused; she did not know how to react to that mysterious call. She was worried as to what was happening. Who was calling and why were they bothering them or him? Bill stepped back in and kissed Sabina on her forehead.

"Do you need anything else? Was breakfast good? Can I get you another cup of coffee?" Bill said as he placed the cellphone down on the table.

Bill grabbed his coffee and walked towards the window to look outside. A text appeared on Bill's phone; she did not want to speak but she could read the caller's name: Gaby. Who the hell was Gaby? Sabina thought she knew about Pat, or Patricia. But who was this Gaby and why was she messing with Bill? Maybe Bill had another girl and he was just playing with her. Sabina could feel all her fears and insecurities coming over her. She kept thinking about this Gaby. Bill turned around and grabbed his cellphone.

"You want to go downstairs? I will need to do a couple of things here before I can join you. Is that ok?" Bill said as he stared at his cellphone.

Sabina did not say anything; she simply walked out and made her way downstairs. She was angry and hurt because she knew in her heart that Bill was playing with her.

"He must think I am a fool. I must be another of his flings." Sabina thought. "Here I am falling in love and he has another girl calling him. Idiot, that is what I am, an idiot" Sabina told herself as she traveled downstairs in the elevator. The elevator stopped on the fourth floor and a man walked in with her.

"Hello, you headed to the convention? What group are you in Gorgeous?" He said Sabina smiled.

"Sabina Goodwin Leadership Team Orange from Tampa" he read out loud.

"Anthony Spanelli, Leadership Team Blue from Atlanta. But my friends call me Tony. I can tell you want to be my friend " Anthony said.

"Nice to meet you," Sabina said.

"So you happy with your group? You stuck with a bunch of service guys? They don't think like we do. I am a Cop in Atlanta, former Marine. I just don't think they do. Not anymore. You want to join our group. I could use some back up" Anthony said with a large smile.

Sabina stood silently as they arrived at the front of the convention. Sabina saw her group and started walking towards them. She then turned towards Anthony and gave him a flirting smile.

"Why don't you join my group and see if you can back me up? Sabina teased.

"Sure thing Babe" Anthony said as they walked together towards her table.

Sabina sat down and Anthony took the liberty to place his hand on her thigh. He began to whisper into her ear and they laughed together. Sabina was forcing herself to tease Anthony. She thought if Bill is going to two-time her, she was going to give him a taste of his own medicine. The ladies at the table looked uncomfortable with Sabina's behavior and Barb was the first to speak up.

"So where is Bill? I thought he was joining us?" Barb asked forcefully.

"Yes he is upstairs; he was getting his girlfriend's phone calls." Sabina said.

"What are you talking about Goodwin?" Kate asked "Aren't you two together?"

"I am not sure anymore," Sabina said.

"Sabina?" Barb said, "You better think about what you are saying"

"I am just trying to enjoy the convention and network with new people," Sabina said.

"Sabina, may I please speak to you? " Bill appeared and stood behind her. He could see that Anthony's hands were all over her.

"Who the hell are you? Babe, you want me to take care of this fool? "Anthony said.

"Sabina, I need to speak to you. Can you please step outside with me?" Bill said again. Anthony stood up and in a second Bill and he were toe-to-toe.

"Sit down Son. This is between Sabina and me. This is none of your business so sit down. Well, Sabina, do you have a moment in private please?" Bill repeated.

"Step back Soldier. I don't want to kick your ass up and down this hallway" Anthony said.

"Once again this is none of your business. Sabina, is this what you want? You want me to hurt this piss ant? Why? He is not worth my time or yours. Now Mr. Spanelli I would recommend you to sit your ass down" Bill said.

"Captain Spanelli Atlanta PD I am also a former Marine and SWAT Team Commander. And I will be happy to show you how we handle things in the street."

"I hate repeating myself, sit your ass down, former Marine. What? You serve a tour and now you are a big guy because you negotiate with a loudspeaker? One tour with the motor pool? Try 17 tours on record and many more to save lives. Sabina please. I will hurt him and it will be your fault" Bill said.

"What the fuck?" Anthony protested.

Sabina stood up and walked outside and Bill began to follow her when Anthony stepped behind them to follow.

"Sit your ass down, dumb ass. Do you know who that guy is?" Barb asked.

"Some soldier that Sabina is screwing" Anthony responded.

"That is the Ghost. He is probably the reason your stupid ass is still alive" Barb said.

"The Ghost from Baghdad? We heard about him when I was in Kuwait. I thought it was a myth. Holy shit that was the Ghost? " Anthony said as he left the table.

Sabina walked to the edge of the hallway while Bill followed her. She stopped abruptly and Bill reached for her but he did not dare touch her.

"Sabina I am not sure what you were thinking? What is going through your head? Did you want me to kill that guy?" Bill said in an angry tone.

"You got some nerve questioning me. I don't owe you any explanation. We are not exclusive. We never said anything about not having fun. I was just having a little convention fling" Sabina said.

"Look Sabina, I know you are scared. I know I have been pushy but I know what I want and what my heart wants. It wants you and only you. I will wait for you. My soul aches for you and my spirit wanders aimlessly without you. I have enough love for both of us and I will wait for you to be ready to accept it. But don't expect me to watch you while you figure it out. I don't deserve to be embarrassed or abused. I love you today, tomorrow and forever." Bill turned her around forcefully and planted a kiss on her that she felt down in her soul. "You get what you want out of your system. Remember I am in your soul. When your spirit quits wandering it will find mine. You are mine and I am yours forever in this world and the next" Bill said and he walked away and disappeared.

"Bill," Sabina said but she could not see herself following him. She was so confused and her head was spinning. Sabina walked back into the convention room and sat down next to Barb.

"What is going on with Bill?" Barb said.

"I don't know Barb," Sabina said.

"Why are you acting so crazy? I thought Bill and you were an item?" Barb asked.

"Bill is a jerk. He was sleeping with me and then getting calls from Gaby. How the hell do you think I should feel?" Sabina said.

"Like an Ass of course. Bill must have been fast-tracked. You think Gaby is a girl? Gaby is the app used to call in Active Units like Bill. I thought he had a few more months or at least weeks. I guess he had to leave right away. You left him like that? You are an Ass. Bill is a catch and you seriously fucked it up. Don't look at me like that girl. If I had an opportunity like yours, Bill would not take off. Foolish pride" Barb said.

"Gaby is not a woman? I am an idiot. What did I do? I need to find Bill. Where is he headed to? You have to help me Barb. Please, I was a jerk. I need to tell him I love him. Please Barb, I know you can help me. Please" Sabina pleaded.

"Oh girl I don't know. You don't understand. He is not sitting at an airport. He was picked up and he is gone. I am not sure where he is headed. It might be Baghdad, Kabul, or anywhere in the Middle East. You don't get how Bill makes a living? He walks among demons to purchase the freedom of soldiers captured before they are beheaded. Bill has a very dangerous job and his head and heart need to be in the right place. I don't know the right thing to do" Barb said, "Okay let me think." Barb said as she took a deep breath," I will help you get a message to him. But the only way is to get a message with his father. Bill's dad is the only one who can contact him, no one else is authorized. I will help you find him and you will need to eat a lot of crow. Come on, let's ditch this party and get you to Wyoming. I need to make some calls while you go upstairs and pack" Barb said.

Sabina walked into the hotel where a few hours ago it was filled with love and life. How could she let it all slip away so easily? She was scared of all that she was feeling alongside Bill, but now she simply felt alone. The room was dark and dreary without his presence. She had lived through his absence, but they were together. She started to fall apart and threw herself on the floor sobbing. "Foolish pride," Sabina told herself.

Within minutes her phone rang, it was Barb,"Get your ass off that floor and come downstairs. I got you a flight to Wyoming and it leaves in 90 minutes. Come on girl, be strong if you want your soldier back you need to fight. Hustle, I got a Lyft en route" Barb yelled out.

# 11

## I Just Called to Say I'm Sorry

SABINA PULLED HERSELF up and ran through her room grabbing her stuff and rushed out. She jumped into the elevator and ran out the front door. Sabina looked around and found Barb waving her over to a black SUV.

"Get to Reagan Airport I will text you your flight information. Do not stop, just get on that plane. I will get you a rental car for Wyoming you just go" Barb said

"Barb I have no words."

"Girl, we will talk later; no time. Safe travels." She hugged Sabina while placing her into the car. "Go!" Barb ordered.

Sabina did not know how she would ever repay Barb for her kindness. She now needed to focus and get to Wyoming. In a matter of minutes she was standing outside of the airport with her carryon luggage in hand.

"Deputy Goodwin?" A tall man asked her, "We have been expecting you. Follow me please" he said.

"What is going on? I need to get to the departure area?" Sabina replied in a confused tone.

"Yes, I am with the TSA. We got a call from Mrs. Barbara Andersen at the Pentagon. We are to personally escort you into the plane without delay. She said it was official business from the Pentagon. So Ma'am please follow me" he replied.

Sabina knew that Barb had clout but she did not realize the importance of her position. Today she was very grateful for her powerful influence. Sabina got into the plane and began praying that she would make it on time to fix up her mess. How could she doubt William? He was straight forward with her and now he would really never know the truth. Sabina looked out of the window and wished the plane would go faster. She needed it to go faster and Sabina needed to speak to Bill. Sabina could feel Bill's touch all over her body and within her soul. She could see the top of the mountains and she wondered how much longer it would take to land. The airport was about an hour from Bill's ranch and Barb did not lie. As Sabina walked through the terminal she got instructions from Barb.

"You should have landed and now you need to make your way to Enterprise Leasing. Your car is rented and ready for you to drive. The address you need is programmed into the GPS. Looks like it is about 45 minutes to an hour from the terminal" Barb texted.

Sabina walked into the car rental and in a matter of minutes she was behind the wheel. 'Holy Crap' she thought Barb had the magic touch. Sabina started the car and made her way towards the ranch. She needed to get her mind and heart right before talking to Bill's dad. She needed his help and Bill needed to know she loved him.

Sabina blasted the radio to clear her head. The first station was playing "To Love Somebody" Sabina started crying as she sang along with Keith Urban "What good does it do if I ain't got you if I ain't got you. You don't know what it's like to love somebody to love somebody."

Sabina could not stop the tears from rolling down her face so she flipped through the stations and she found their song. She recalled how just the other night she and Bill were walking in D.C and riding the Ferris wheel. Bill with his broken voice began singing their song,

**I can dream about you.** For Sabina the lyrics were telling their story and she could feel

Bill's spirit lingering around. She was getting closer to the property and she could see the

beauty of the territory. As the moonlight guided her through the final turn all Sabina could see

was the fencing and green pastures. Sabina loved the area at first sight and she could see all the

care and attention he has dedicated to his portion of Mother Earth.  Sabina pulled over and she

could see the Moonlight kissing the top of the roof. She gathered that it was the main house and

Sabina made her way towards the house.

Bill's house was all that she imagined and then some. Amazing, she thought. The house

was a log cabin with a wraparound porch. There were two wooden rocking chairs carved out of

oak with pillows that read Welcome. She looked around and she could see Bill's touch in

everything she noticed and as she touched it she could feel Bill's energy. Sabina took a big deep

breath and calmed herself down before she tapped on the door. Two knocks was all it took for

his Dad to open the door.

"Good Evening are you Bill's, I mean William Young's father?" Sabina asked with a

shaken voice.

"You must be Billie's ray of sunshine. Come on in child I was expecting you. The storm

clouds told me that there was trouble between you two. I know Billie got called in and he is

headed to his sandbox. Why are you here? What troubles you child?" he asked.

"I need your help. I don't know how much time there is but I need to get a message to

Bill. I need to tell him that I love him. I need to tell him I was wrong and he needs to know the

truth." Sabina began to tear up, "Please help me." Sabina said as she fell into Bill's Dad's arms.

"I could feel the storms brewing, I told Billie to take it easy and slow with you. Your

type of love is combustible with just a breeze. Today, I was in the field and my mustang took me to the creek at the top of a ridge. I followed his instinct and when I got there I saw a white buffalo. Buffalos are sacred symbols of our people but particularly white ones are signs. White buffalos bring prosperity and good luck. They are extremely rare and this one was a baby. As I took in the sight I could also see red clouds forming in the east. You are passion and ice and my Billie is thunder and water. Combined you two can bring beauty and danger. You must have been really frightened when Billie opened his heart to you. I know his mother was when I showed her that my heart and spirit found hers. Our love made the earth shake and even skip a beat. I can only imagine that you two did the same. We can talk more later and you came for my help. This old man can tell long stories and waste time. Let me see if I can get that message to him before he lands in the sands" he said.

"I don't know if there is enough time. It might be too late and he will not know how I really feel" Sabina said with tears in her eyes. They stood outside and Bill's father looked at the sky and said to the moon "let the light guide your spirit and it will bring Bill's soul home. Let's go inside and I will find that phone number. I have to call the satellite phone and he will get a link so you can see each other" he said as they walked into the beautiful home. Sabina followed him into the office and watched him slowly dial a number. Seconds later the computer alerted him to a link. He looked at Sabina with kindness in his eyes and said, "Anytime now Billie will be able to see you. Deep breath child he will be here in a few seconds."

The computer began to ring like a telephone with static on the line and within seconds Bill could see his father's image coming into his screen. "Billie, it's Dad. Billie are you there? Son, can you hear me? Billie, it's Dad" he said repeatedly. There was a long pause Sabina was on edge and could only pray to see if they were actually connected. And then she could hear.

"Pops, Pops I am here. I am so glad you called. I need your guidance. I think I lost my Sunshine forever." Static and then connected to Bill's voice shouting "Pops! Pops! Can you hear me? Please can you hear me?" Bill said.

"Son, Sabina is here, she is here. You did not lose her. She is here with me. Hold on" he signaled Sabina to come to the front of the computer screen.

"Sunshine, is that really you? You are in Wyoming with my Dad? What are you doing there? How did you get there?" Bill said with laughter in his voice.

"William, William, do you still love me?" She asked while holding back her tears.

"Forever and forever more" Bill responded.

"Bill I am so sorry I don't know what I was thinking or doing. I was scared and confused. I am not scared anymore. I need you to know that I love you and I will love you forever. William, please forgive me please. I need you" Sabina said but she could not hold her tears back.

"Sunshine, Sunshine you are mine and I am yours forever. Forever more I promise. I thought I had lost you and pushed you away. Please forgive me for my abruptness, but I cannot contain my love for you" Bill said as the connection became faint.

"William, William don't go. I love you. Do you hear me? I love you and I cannot live without you. I just found you. I cannot lose you please Bill. Can you hear me?" Sabina said.

"Sunshine, do you still love me?" Bill said loud and clear "we only had a few minutes before we get disconnected, so tell me Sunshine: do you still love me? Bill teased.

"Forever and forever more William I will always love you" Sabina responded.

"Sabina, I wish I was there. I want to hold you and make sure you know that you are safe. If you say yes I will make sure you are happy and safe every second of your life. Our spirits are already together. Now all that is needed is for you to open your heart and say "yes." Sunshine, will you marry me?" Bill asked.

"William, I love you and I cannot imagine not being with you. Yes, I will be your wife on this earth and wherever our spirits take us. Bill, I love you today and forever" Sabina said as Bill's Dad handed her a small wooden box and she opened it.

"Bill its lovely," she said.

"It was my mother's ring and her mother's ring before that. It has been in my family for generations and their love has endured and survived this world and into the next" Bill explained. "Sunshine, do you still love me?" Bill teased.

"Forever and forever more William! I love you and I cannot wait until you come home to me. Come home to me Bill please, promise me that you will come back to me" Sabina said.

"Sunshine I promise and when we get back we will get married. You are my sunshine. I will come home to you, I promise" Bill said as the signal faded away and they were disconnected.

# 12

## A Promise of Forever

NOW ALL SABINA could do was stare at her ring and smile at the promise of her future. The ring was an impressive piece of art. A white gold ring that held spotted diamonds crafted to resemble the Globe. Every stone was braided with an elegant and distinct feature to tell a story. Sabina embraced her beautiful gem and thought of Bill's mother and grandmother and how much love this one ring had brought to them. She felt humble to know Bill loved her to such an extent to trust her with the ring but that this abundance of love was theirs to call their own. Sabina was feeling complete when she heard a light knocking on the door.

"Child are you alright?" Bill's Dad said while he was peeking into the room.

"Oh, Mr. Young, I am so sorry. Yes, everything is perfect. Thank you so much for your kindness and help. I really have no words" Sabina spilled out all her words quickly as she began to stand up.

"Ah," he said with a huge smile similar to Bill's "so you said yes and now you are one of us. Welcome to our family child, I guess I better introduce myself or Billie will have me for lunch. I am Benjamin Young, son of Walking Bear and Esmeralda. My father was a full blooded Cherokee Indian. My mother, Esmeralda, was the daughter of a Cherokee maiden and an Irishman. Billie's bloodline is rich in tradition and passion. He loves with all his heart, spirit, body, and mind. Billie loves you and his spirit is guided by his mother's love. I know you are his other half and no one should mess with the spirit world. Let's get you settled in for the night. Come, come, you can stay in Billie's room. I can get you something to eat or drink. Come on, come follow me I will show you the bedroom. You can get some rest and I can show you the ranch in the morning." Sabina followed Ben as he led her upstairs to the Master Bedroom door.

"I will be in my house up the road. If you need anything you can call on the intercom system. Billie wanted it that way because he says I am getting up in years. I want my independence and he wants to make sure I care for myself. So we had a compromise and he installed the system and every night we say goodnight and dream of our loves" Ben said with a kind smile. "Anyway this is your home Child we will talk in the morning and figure it all out. You rest and recover; you had a long emotional day. Rest your spirit. Billie knows you love him. He loves you. We will talk in the morning" Ben said as he opened the bedroom door. "Oh, Wolf. I forgot to introduce you to Wolf. He is inside of Billie's room. Wolf, come meet Sabina and give her a proper greeting."

From the corner of the room came a sheepdog that resembled a wolf. Wolf was a large dog who held his 80 pound muscular frame with dignity and royalty. Wolf came over and sniffed Sabina and circled her. He was an impressive animal and Sabina almost felt accosted by this inspection. "Relax he is just making sure you are a friend" Ben said as the dog finished and then walked back into the bedroom. "He says you are good. Go on in and rest Wolf will take care of you. Wolf sleeps inside of Billie's room for a couple of days until he gets used to the idea that he is gone. He misses Billie and cries for him. Wolf showed up one day and he quickly became Billie's faithful companion. I think they choose one another" Ben said. Sabina walked into the bedroom and dropped her bag on the floor.

Wolf sat next to the bed until Sabina settled herself into the bed. She was exhausted and needed to rest. She could smell Bill's scent all over the room and his pillow. She knew he was present with her in spirit. Sabina was filled with joy and she could not contain it. As her face rolled over his pillow she could imagine him with her. Sabina told herself not to be an idiot, Bill, her William, was the one. She could no longer stand fast and she accepted his love. She was ready and needed to happily accept the invitation into his life. Sabina was finally content and her heart was filled.

Tonight she would rest and dream with Bill and their future lives together. Sabina woke up to the smell of crispy bacon and eggs, biscuits, and coffee. Oh Lord, she needed that first cup of coffee. She had slept in one of Bill's shirts and she did not think it was appropriate to come out wearing his clothes. She decided to dress but all she had with her was one pair of jeans and t-shirt. She rushed to get ready and threw over a blue shirt Bill had hanging in his closet. I hope he doesn't mind she thought but I need to look somewhat together for his dad. She stepped into the kitchen to find Bill's father covered in flour. She smiled as she reached for her first cup of coffee.

"Good Morning my Child, I was so excited to make your breakfast the bag slipped out of my hands. So much for first impressions ha?" Ben said while they both began to laugh. Ben's laughter reminded her of Bill. It was a laughter that made your heart skip a beat and filled the room with joy. The food was fantastic, just what Sabina needed to start her day. She helped clean up the mess in the kitchen and then they headed outside for the grand tour of the ranch. As Sabina stepped outside she could see the grandeur of the property which had green valleys and the mountains as a background.

"This place is breathtaking," she said.

"This is the land of my people. My ancestors roamed this area for centuries before the white man made their way across. Billie and I wanted to keep as much of the traditions as possible. We welcomed all like the Spirit Winds taught us. We have Mustangs, Buffalo, Hawks, Bear, and Deer. All creatures get along with us and we get along with them. Balance is what makes this place successful. Come let me guide you through the property, can you ride?" Ben asked.

"Yes, I know how to ride a horse," Sabina answered with pride.

"This is Peanut, he is gentle and he will take you on your tour. Just be mindful of what you feel because he will feel it as well. Some of the terrain is uneven and you will have to trust him" Ben said as he helped her startle Peanut.

# 13

## This Land is Our Land

"LET ME START from the beginning. I am Benjamin, the only son of Standing Bear. Standing Bear was a direct descendant of Sequoia, who invented the first written language from my people, the Cherokee. Our people are proud, prosperous, and kind. During the time that White people call The Trail of Tears many tribes were relocated to our lands here. Among them came a young maiden, Esmeralda, daughter of a Navaho and an Irish Calvary soldier. Many did not accept Esmeralda, since God made her beautiful. She had green eyes and olive skin with delicate white features like thin lips, and a small frame. She looked like a baby doll and the women were jealous of her and called her half-breed or a mute. They would throw rocks and mud at her if she came near them and was then forced to live at the edge of the reservation away from everyone. She hid during the day to avoid the angry mob and cried for her tribe to find her."

Ben said as he took a deep breath as if he was remembering Esmeralda and then he continued,

"Every night she would go out and do her chores, wash, gather food, and walk in the moonlight. One day she was taking a bath in the river when Standing Bear saw her in the moonlight. His spirit jumped out of his body and went towards hers. She was the vision he had been looking for and he could no longer live without her. Esmeralda heard someone coming towards her and she hid. For the next seven days Standing Bear waited for her at the edge of the water. He was not sure if she was real or just a vision, but he was not taking any chances. On the seventh day Esmeralda came to the river's edge and sat next to him. Their hands touched and their spirits united."

"Soon Standing Bear and Esmeralda were married and anyone who stood in their way were reminded that this marriage was blessed by Sequoia himself, a half-breed, the son of an Army Cavalry Soldier and the daughter of a Cherokee Princess. Their union was told in the stars and no one ever dared to call Esmeralda a half- breed again. My Billie loves that story and I tell it to him every time he asks me about his grandparents. True love is suffering and to reach happiness. I was happy with Billie's mother who left this earth too soon. Now I wait for her to come to me every night at the edge of the river. One day she and I will be together, but I talk too much and tell too many stories. Let's stop her and rest the horses for a minute" Ben requested.

Sabina did not even notice that they had reached the river's edge because she had been so engrossed in Ben's story. She was fascinated with their history, the people, and she wanted to hear more. She wanted to know all about William and his people. But she stopped Peanut and dismounted without any assistance. They walked to the edge of the river and Ben told her about fishing as a boy in the waters, and teaching Bill to be carefree in this area.  Sabina absorbed all the tails, stories, and laughter Ben was providing. She was so happy and at peace to be welcomed by him into Bill's tribe. Sabina finally found the family she was missing and her heart was mending as her fears and self-doubt were washed away.

"I love this river, you know it brings back memories of my great love. You and Billie have something special, but his Mama and I well know that love was out of this world. It is what I hope for you and Billie to have. Come Child, make this old man happy and let me tell you about my Willow. Yes, Billie's mom was a special person. She was brave as she was beautiful.

Fearless as she was cautious and when she gave her heart much like my Billie she gave it all. We met on this river but on the other side of the mountain. I caught her bathing in the hot springs which have healing powers. She was a sight, a tan woman with these piercing green eyes that could read your soul. I was captivated by her beauty immediately, but that was one stubborn creature. No matter what I did, she would not look at me. I think her pride was hurt because I had seen her vulnerable and naked. I had to work hard to tame her spirit.

One day I walked up to her and said, "Willow I love you and if you don't love me I got enough love for both of us. If you marry me, I will keep you warm during the cold nights. I promise you will not ever want for anything. If you will have me, I will be at your side in this world and the next. She looked at me and said, 'Ben, what has taken you so long to come to me? I have been waiting for you.' She smiled and then said, 'Yes, if you will have me I will be with you in this world and the next.' Oh that woman drove me crazy and I loved her each day more and more.

Willow was Navajo and her people were visionaries. She is the one that told me she would only be with me until the spirit world called her. So I made it my mission to make her happy each day. Billie was her life and I lived for my Willow. I knew our time together on this planet was going to be short." Ben turned away to hide his tears and took a deep breath and then continued, "My Willow was only on this Earth for 30 years, but she gave me the two greatest gifts: Billie and the promise that one day we'll be together forever.

Willow was diagnosed with cancer and there was nothing we could do for her. She had suffered for a long time without seeking treatment. She never told me she was not feeling well until one day the pain was too much. I took her to Denver and we were told it was too late to save her life so I brought her home. I guess Billie was about 10 years old then. We spent the day together, all three of us. I dropped Billie off with family and Willow and I went to find our hot spring. It was a lovely night we spent together wrapped up in a blanket on the edge of the springs. I could see the storm clouds rolling across the hill when my Willow left me. But I keep her promise in my heart and soon we will be together in the next world. So now I wait for my storm clouds to take me away" Ben cleared his tears and looked at Sabina.

"His mother blesses your union. My Billie needs someone like you to love him on this earth and the next. Come let's head back before I bore you to death with my old Indian stories" Ben said.

"Don't stop, I want to know everything about Bill. Please tell me more" Sabina pleaded as she remounted Peanut. They headed back while Ben continued with a new part of Bill's history.

"Willow was my white buffalo. Do you know of the legend of the white buffalo Child?" Ben asked. "For our people white buffalo are sacred symbols and my Willow was mine much like you are Billie's. The legend tells how the People had lost their ability to communicate with the Creator. So the Creator sent a scared creature a white Buffalo to teach the People how to pray by smoking a sacred pipe. The white buffalo was a woman who many warriors lusted for, however, none of them came with a pure heart. She would transform herself into a cloud of dust and disappear. She roamed the Earth looking for a respectful hunter who was willing to tame his desire until she was transformed into a maiden by his love. My Willow was transformed and now you are as well.  Come,  I will tell you another story later when we are home." Sabina looked up and they had made it back to the house without her noticing the distance they had covered.

"What should I call you?" Sabina asked.

"What does your heart tell you?" Ben responded.

"Papa. I'd like to call you Papa if that is alright."

"My Child I would love that. Why don't you rest for a bit and I will come back after I settle the horses and check on the ranch? If you want anything let me know. Make yourself at home. I will be back in a couple of hours" Ben said as he rode away while pulling Peanut behind him.

Sabina walked on the porch admiring the view and hoped this was not a dream. "God if this is a dream I don't want to wake up ever." Sabina said as she was caught by Wolf who seemed to be reading her mind. "Ok Wolf, let's check out the inside of my new home." Sabina walked in to take a good look at Bill's house. She was so curious to know everything about him.

# 14

## The Blood of Our Fathers

A FEW HOURS later Ben was standing at the doorway asking her, "You hungry my Child?"

"I shared a sandwich with Wolf. I am ok but can I fix you anything? How about some coffee?" Sabina asked as she handed him his cup. As she watched him enjoy the coffee he could see that there was something she was dying to ask.

"What is it my Child? What are you itching to know?" Ben asked.

"I see the pictures and war metals on the wall in Bill's office. Who are those people?" Sabina asked with some hesitation.

"Oh my Child, you are joining a family of warriors. My Willow's family were the first WindTalkers. You see during World War II the White man came to the Navajo people for help. The Japanese were a great enemy and they had deciphered every code the White man had. The language of the Navajo was used to save many a mission. And our people were so brave that they would have rather sacrificed themselves than give up information to the enemy. That is the blood that runs through Billie's veins. The pictures and metals tell the story of how our people tried to keep the White man safe. Billie learned all about them and the fire inside of him was too much to be contained.  The night he told me he was enlisting I asked him why? Billie said, 'Remember what you taught me Pops, what the Great Spirit said to the first warrior. The Great Spirit told him his purpose was to fight for his tribe, family, and the brothers you meet along the way. In other words, fight for your own and not for the Great Spirit.' He joined the Army and has been going strong for almost two decades now.  I really wanted him not to join. I wanted him to have another type of life, but who was I to stop Billie? I enlisted too. I had the same quest from the Great Spirit and I too serve to save all of the Creator's creatures" Ben said as he fought off his tears.

"I hope soon with you here that he will find peace and will no longer need to serve. Billie has done his part and from what I know so have you. My child you have kept many strangers safe and now it is time for you two to be at peace. To be together and enjoy one another. Come let's see what Billie left at the house. You should have more than a sandwich. He will kill me if I don't take good care of you."

# 15

# One Night in the Hot Springs

THEY SPENT THE remainder of the day talking about life at the ranch and Sabina told Ben about her family and her traditions. These days came and went between horse riding and long walks. The day before she was to head back to Florida, Ben took Sabina to the hot springs so she could heal and rest. He explained to her that the natural warm water would soothe her soul and calm all her fears. Sabina could not argue that she needed something to make her feel less anxious. After Ben left she disrobed and got into the natural tub of warm water. She immediately felt a calmness come over her body.

Every fear and inhibition was lifted with each breath she took. Sabina found herself drifting off to sleep and she began to dream of the warm water surrounding her as Bill's arms. It's so peaceful and beautiful here. Sabina could see herself living in this place, surrounded with good energy and loving hearts. Maybe her dream of raising a family would really come true: she was so lucky she found Bill, or had they found one another? Was it written? Was it fate?

Every evening Sabina would take long walks along the path, or broken path, when one day she came upon a foggy area. She had to adjust her eyes and realized it was a hot spring in the shape of a tub. She had heard about these but never saw them in real life. Sabina took off her clothes since there was no one around and lowered herself in the tub. The heat against her skin felt soothing. Being here felt like it could be paradise except she was missing her Bill. She closed her eyes and imagined Bill walking towards her at the very moment the water pressures were making her body tingle in all the places she wanted Bill to touch. He was taking off his shirt which pleased her roaming eyes and then when he took off his jeans, her roaming fingers were strumming the sweet spot where she most wanted Bill.

A far away wolf was howling and woke her from her daydream. Sabina's spirit was abruptly interrupted and forced to return to her present by Wolf who was howling at the moon.

She did not realize how quickly time had passed and she needed to make her way back home. Bill's house was now her house and she needed to go back to Florida just to make all the arrangements. Sabina finally accepted her destiny and that was to be with Bill on this earth and in the next forever. "William, William forever and forever more" Sabina said out loud as she got dressed.

This was the last night she would be at Bill's house and she wanted to ensure that Ben knew she had accepted her destiny. She tried to call him on the intercom system with no success. Sabina stepped outside and she could see him closing the large barn doors. She walked towards him and called out, "Papa are you good? Do you need help?"

"No, My Child, just the age got me and I am running behind in my chores. I heard Wolf out there with you. He must have seen Bill's spirit joining yours. I am happy for you both. I will sleep with a smile in my heart" he said "Good night then safe travels in the morning."

Sabina had to walk away; she was almost embarrassed about her behavior in the woods. She was sure no one had seen her except maybe Wolf and now she was sure he had snitched. Sabina walked quickly inside and gave him a look that made Wolf run into the bedroom as if to hide and find refuge if Bill was there. Sabina then grabbed him by the ears and kissed him. "Wolf, you better stop tattling on me." She laughed and prepared herself for bed and her trip in the morning.  Sabina had a number of things to prepare once she landed back in Florida. She did her best to get some rest and get back into the real world and get ready for her new life.

# 16

**Heading South**

AS SHE DROVE away from Bill's ranch she waved at Ben who was riding into the prairie when her cell phone rang with an unidentifiable number.

"Hello," Sabina said.

"Hey there Ms. Florida, it's Barb. You got a second?" Barb said.

"Of course, Barb, I have so much to tell you. I was going to call you once I got to the airport." Sabina responded.

"So how did things work out with your Soldier Hot Body? You guys good or did you let yourself get in the way again. I swear Sabina if you fucked this up I will kick you square in the ass" Barb said, "I am so sorry I get emotional about these things. But how did it go?"

"It went well. Now that is a lie. It was and is extraordinary. Bill asked me to marry him and I said." Sabina could not get the last word out when she heard Barb yelling and screaming.

"Yes! Yes! Yes I am fucking amazing. I knew that you two were perfect for one another."

"So I am heading to Florida. I got some things to square away before I can get back here. Bill is doing a six-week mission and that gives me time to get started in the relocation process" Sabina said.

"Great news Babe, blessings and more blessings. You guys are perfect for one another. So glad to hear both of you are on the right track" Barb said but was quickly interrupted by Sabina,

"Barb I have no words to thank you. Really if it wasn't for your kindness I would not have made it. Thank you, thank you" Sabina said.

"You are so welcome girl! Listen I also wanted you to know that I took it upon myself to have Bill's unit assigned to me. I am going to keep an eye out for you two" Barb said.

"What does that mean Barb? I don't understand. I thought you worked for the Pentagon. What do you have to do with Army Intelligence?" Sabina asked in an inquisitive tone.

"Oh I forget; you're a civilian. Well I never told you what I do for the Pentagon, but let's say it's a matter of national security. And to that end, Bill is a matter of national security" Barb replied.

"Wow Barb I did not know you had that much power. I did not see that coming" Sabina said.

"I am like nitroglycerin, small but mighty.  Look, I got to head to another meeting. But I will let you know how your soldier is doing in the sandbox. See you soon Doll. Oh, and send me that wedding invite, I will be there" Barb said in a rush and the phone disconnected.

# 17

## A Season of Waiting

IT WAS NOT long before Sabina settled into her seat and she found herself arriving in Orlando. Soon after she found herself at her ranch figuring out what steps she had to take to make her move. Sabina sent out an email to Human Resources and then had a better understanding of how to handle her changes. Early in the morning she met with Human Resources and then was told she had a meeting with the Sheriff.  She stepped into his office and had her resignation in mind, but he had other plans.  The Sheriff was surprised that she wanted

to resign or retire whichever was easier for the department.

The sheriff gave Sabina the best option he could possibly have for her future. He asked

if she was willing to stay as a Reserve Deputy until he managed to replace her if she still

wanted to relocate full time. The sheriff stated he had been getting reports of civil unrest around

the country and he feared the mess was heading to Florida. He explained to Sabina that she

would assist with mass calls for service, parades, and other needs for the county. Sabina thought

for a minute and she agreed to be a Reserve Deputy until he could fill her spot. Her

reassignment seemed to be an easy transition for everyone which took a simple matter of

weeks.

Sabina decided not to sell her parent's home but rather allow Sophia and her husband to

manage the property as well as the bakery. She wanted to contribute to Bill's ranch, but she also

wanted to keep her parents' memory alive. Sabina was happy with her decision and now it was

just a waiting game to see how to take the next step. She really enjoyed her new place in the

world and was enjoying every minute of each day.

She was coming off an easy shift. Sabina had been assigned to work with the Special

Olympics Coordinator and it was a very fulfilling day. She stepped out of the shower to find she

had missed a call from Barb. Her heart skipped a beat when she saw the missed call and text

message that simply read "911 call Barb." Sabina took a deep breath before she dialed and then

called.

"Hey girl, I have to tell you that Bill is in trouble. I have been tracking his unit and

something went terribly wrong. He was helping move a unit when the convoy was hit and

attacked. We are looking at a number of casualties and deaths. Bill is not among them but I

think he might have been captured. The hummer was struck multiple times and last reports say he was seen pulling a fellow soldier out from the wreckage when they were overtaken by the enemy. I wish I had better news for you. I know he is alive but that is all. We are searching for him and I promise you we will not leave him behind" Barb reported.

"Barb, what do I do?" Sabina said, trying not to cry.

"Pray! Pray hard, but I promise you he is alive. He has an implant with a tracking device and I see his blood pressure, temperature and heart rate. He is alive. Now I have to find him to bring him home to you. So pull yourself together and let me see if I can trace his cute, little butt" Barb said, trying to keep Sabina calm.

"Barb, please bring him home safe" Sabina said.

"You pray girl. Now, let me work. I promise you if I get anything I will let you know. Just trust me. I have several tracking devices on his tail. It is just a matter of getting them in the right grid and then we will go in guns blazing for him. I will bring your William home come Hell or High Water. Bill will be back for you. Okay. Gotta go, Doll" Barb said as she hung up the phone.

Sabina went outside and looked at the sky and noticed the clouds becoming dark. It was Florida and the weather at times is unpredictable, but today seemed dark and overcast. She thought of Ben's words and how he could read trouble brewing in the skies. Sabina wondered if she could read what the weather was trying to tell her, but she could only feel a pain in her heart and an ache in her soul. Sabina knew Bill's job was dangerous but she did not expect to be drowning in fear and desperation from not knowing if he was safe. She kept looking at the sky and praying for news, good news, that Bill no longer was MIA, Missing in Action. "Oh God, please bring him home safely" Sabina pleaded as she bowed her head.

The hours became days and days were quickly transforming into weeks and Sabina did not have any news. She finally understood the connection between her and Bill. And she was missing him. Not getting any information was simply agony. Sabina told herself she was going to wait just one more hour and then she was calling Barb. Barb had to give her something and at this point Sabina just needed to break the silence. She then began the long extensive argument with the clock. I will call at four she would say, and then walk into another room. Once there, Sabina would turn her attention to something to distract herself and somehow find a clock and tell herself, "Ok I will call in 50 minutes. That is it, I will just wait." This ceremony kept going for over 30 minutes when she heard her cell phone ring. "Please God, let it be good news!"

"Hello," Sabina said.

"Doll, it's Barb. How are you holding up? Do you need anything?" Barb kindly said.

"Barb, I need to know something. Can you please tell me anything? I need to know Bill is alright. Anything? Anything at all? I am going crazy not knowing anything. Please Barb, give me something. Give me hope" Sabina pleaded while tears were rolling down her face.

"Look Doll, all I can tell you is that he is alive. I can tell that for sure and we are searching for him. He is alive; I promise you" Barb said.

"Barb, I feel like I can't breathe without him. How do you live through this? I swear the not knowing is what is killing me."

"Sabina, I will not give you false hope. But he is alive and I will find him for you. You got to trust me. I know it has been a couple of weeks since we last spoke, but we are searching for him" Barb insisted.

"Can you tell me where he is? What country? What region? Anything?" Sabina asked.

"I can tell you he was doing his job and William is really good at this job. He is trapped somewhere behind enemy lines. Which enemy and in what region I cannot tell you. He is in the Middle East and, as you well know, our country has many enemies in that part of the world. We also have a lot of allies and good people around us. So, keep the faith. He is alive and as long as he is fighting, you need to fight for him as well. Stay strong. I will call you as soon as I am able to" Barb said. "Oh and remember he is alive" Barb said before disconnecting.

Sabina fell to her knees and began sobbing. She could feel the pain in her heart as the helplessness overcame her. She wanted to run towards him; she desperately wanted to help search for Bill. Now, all she could do was pray and wait for him to make it home. Sabina never felt so alone in her life. She recalled Barb's words the last time she found herself crying on the floor. "Get up. Do something! Get up now!" She decided to text Barb quickly and tell her she was heading back to Wyoming. Sabina was determined right then and there to wait for the news, any news, with Ben. He was now her family and was alone at the ranch. Together they would pray and hope and soon enough they would get some sort of news. She prepared for the trip, packed what she needed and, in a matter of hours, Sabina found herself driving to Wyoming. It was a 30-hour drive so she would drive until she needed rest and then continue. She wanted to have family around her so sleep was not essential at this time.

# 18

## The Road Home

SABINA ARRIVED AT Bill's ranch to find Ben waiting, sitting on the porch. She was dead tired and all she could do was fall into his embrace.

"I didn't know what to do and all I could think of was to come home," Sabina said.

"Come my child. We will wait for Billie together. I am happy you are home" Ben helped Sabina inside. He prepared her a small meal and gave her a warm cup of tea. "Get some rest now. Go on, Wolf will wait for you. Don't worry my child, bad news travels fast. We just need to keep the faith that The Creator will smile upon Billie and bring him home. Don't worry he is alive, I can feel it in my bones. Soon after you rest, you will see I am right. Now rest and dream we will get good news soon enough" Ben said.

"How can you be so certain?" Sabina asked.

"I see the clouds clearing and the dust lifting. I got faith in Billie. I raised him to be a warrior and in my heart I know he is fighting to get back to you. Hold fast to your love and believe. Billie's Spirit is here telling me he is alive" Ben replied.

Ben waited until Sabina had fallen asleep and he stepped outside to watch the clouds go by. He sat there admiring the vastness of the skies, the twinkle of each star and waves of breeze that seemed to dispel the clouds above the Eastern Territory. "Ah" he said as he raised his arms to embrace the sky, "My son, you are safe. Stay in the fight. I got your girl here with me and she is safe. Come home soon, Billie, we are waiting for you. Oh Creator, I will pray to you as you have taught me. Father of our fathers, bring Billie home safe. Let his spirit return to him so he can guide us to his body.

The next morning Sabina woke to find Wolf pouncing on her. She did not know what was going on but she quickly dressed and stepped outside. Wolf ran off into the prairie as she stood on the porch wondering what on earth was happening.

"You feel better, my child? Did you get any rest?" Ben asked while sitting on the porch.

"Oh, yes, thank you Papa. Did you sleep out here all night?" Sabina inquired.

"My soul was tired of wandering around. I found Billie in my travels. He is with his friend and they are covered in sand, but don't worry, they are alive and fighting to get home. He said they will be rescued soon. He wanted me to tell you not to give up on him" Ben said in a weak tone.

"Never. Bill is my forever" Sabina said, "Thank you for taking me in. I know you could have turned me away last night, but I needed to be here."

"My Child, you belong here and this will always be your home. Come, let's greet the day. I need to go and pay my debt with the Spirit world. I will need to go and smoke the pipe like the white buffalo taught us" Ben said.

"What should I do?" Sabina asked.

"I will teach you to pray our way. Come, it will help clear the way for Billie to find his way home."

Ben and Sabina reached the ridge and were looking down at what could only be described as the center of the world. Where they stood one could see the river below rushing underneath the mountain peak. Near the junction was a gravel flat site.

"This is our land's sacred spot. I come here for ceremony and prayer. First thing's first, let me teach you. Humans can lose the balance between giving and taking. These ceremonies seek to clear their path. The prayers for world renewal tell the Spirit people where we are going and what we need from them."

Ben took Sabina's arms and raised them to the skies. "We say, listen Mountain. You explain the acts as you perform them. Spirit people are creatures of supernatural aspects which include anything from mountains to people. We humans are the worst of the Spirit people because we have the shortest memory. The prayer then is a reminder to people of their obligations to the other Spirit people." Ben then walked back to the gravel site and began making a circle with a variety of rocks. "Come, come help me, my Child. We will light the flames here and call upon our Spirits to help Billie."

Sabina watched the low flames dance as Ben fueled them with sage and other herbs. He then began telling her about the story of the buffalo stone. He explained during a rough winter in deep snow, the Cherokee found themselves out of food. As the sun set, the young wife of the Chief went looking for firewood. As she made her way to the river, she heard chirping from a tree. In a fork in the tree there was a stone. The stone gave her songs. "Teach your elders to sing these songs," it said, and I will provide for all of you. That night, the Elders came to the tipi. Everyone was faint with hunger but still sang songs. A storm came up, burying the tipis in snow. But when families dug themselves out the next morning, they saw buffalo walking through the camp. My Child, today we pray in the words of our ancestors and send this smoke to my son and your love, for him to be home soon." Ben ended the ceremony by blowing sage over them both and sprinkling water from the river over the flames.

They got back on their horses and made their way to the ranch. Sabina saw Wolf pacing back and forth on the porch. "What is he doing, Papa? He has been goofy all day. Do you know what he is trying to tell us? Sabina asked. Ben did not have a response. But Wolf was doing the same thing the following evening. He simply would not sit still. Wolf walked back and forth and simply would not eat. When Sabina let him out he would run into the prairie and then come back hours later. Finally, Sabina could not worry about him as well so she decided to try to keep him on the porch. Wolf started whining again; he wanted out and she ordered him to stay with her. Sabina assumed he would protest but he did not. Wolf just sat next to her. Sabina began looking at the sky when she noticed a car pulling into the ranch.

The black sedan pulled right in front of the house. Sabina was on edge; she feared it was the military Chaplin making the final notification. She watched carefully as a tall slender female in a Marine uniform walked out of the car and began to approach her.  Sabina took a deep breath as Wolf ran off the porch and knocked the girl over and began licking her face. Sabina was stunned and she had a hard time calling Wolf off. She decided to yell for Ben "Papa, Papa come quick."

Ben ran up towards Wolf and called him off with a whistle.

"I am so sorry Officer, I don't know what came over him" Sabina said as she was trying to help the female up.

"Wolf is just saying hello. You must be Bill's Sunshine. I am Ellie, Ellis Francis Walker.  Bill's like my older brother. Bill took my older brother's place when he was killed in action in Kuwait. Scott and Bill went to boot camp together. They were buddies. They had each other's back till the end. They promised one another to take care of their families if anything happened. Bill had a wife, now his ex-wife, and his wonderful father. Scott just had me, since we had no other family. When Scott was killed, Bill took me under his wing. He came to all my games, concerts, and graduations. Bill was not happy when I decided to join up, but he supported me. Then when I got into a jam with some idiot, Bill was there to help me. So, you see, we are family and when we are in trouble family comes together. I would have been here weeks ago but I was stuck and I just got my leave approved.  So what do we know?" Ellie said.

"Nice to meet you Ellie. I am Sabina. We are still waiting to hear something, anything" Sabina said.

"Don't worry, we will. I promise you it will be soon. Come, Ellie, let's get you in the house. Wolf has been waiting for you" Ben responded.

"I hope you don't mind, Sabina. I just thought I could keep you company while we wait. I should have called first. I am sorry" Ellie said.

"Don't be sorry!! Come on in! I have a pot of coffee ready and I can make you something to eat. Don't worry. Let's grab your gear and get you settled in" Sabina said.

"Sabina, Bill told me that if anything happened to him, I needed to come home and take care of you" Ellie said.

"Take care of me? Boy, Bill has some nerve. Wait till I get my arms around him" Sabina said. "Ellie, thank you so much for coming home. I am so glad you are here."

Ellie walked in with Ben and Sabina. As they were sitting and catching up, Wolf started to act peculiar again. He was pacing, and running to the door and then jumping on the furniture. "Ellie, do you know what he is trying to tell us?" Sabina asked. Wolf then sat in front of her cell phone.

"Sabina, is your phone ringing?" Ellie asked.

"Let me check. Wait, it's a text message with a link. It's from Barb" Sabina said as they walked into the office and linked up. In a matter of seconds, Barb was on the screen talking to her.

"Hey Doll, pack your bags I found your soldier. We got Bill, he is safe" Barb said with much enthusiasm.

"Bill? you got Bill? Is he safe? Barb, thank you, thank you, thank you" Sabina responded.

"We got him a couple hours ago. I had to clear some things before getting you notified. Yes, he is safe. But you understand he and another soldier were captured for weeks. He is pretty weak and beaten up. Doll, we got them both safe and they are stable" Barb said.

"Barb, you are amazing, thank you. I have no words to tell you how grateful I am. You found my Bill" Sabina said.

"Doll, Doll, listen he is in the hospital and we are transferring him well, both of them, to Bethesda Maryland Naval Hospital. So pack your bags in the morning and I will get you there" Barb instructed.

"Barb, Ellie is here and I would like her to go with me if possible" Sabina asked.

"Ellie, Bill's baby sister. Of course, I will get you both there, no problem." Barb responded.

"Barb, you are amazing," Sabina replied.

"Listen Doll, I do need to prepare you.  Bill is fine but he took a beating and he might suffer from Post-Traumatic Stress. The guys were tortured and traumatized. They were left in a dried up well for weeks. I just don't want you to be scared if he doesn't look or act like your Bill. He needs time to heal and he needs you at his side" Barb cautioned.

"I understand Barb," Sabina said.

"Ok then, I will try to make the trip to Maryland to catch up with you guys, but no promises. It looks like things are unraveling here in the home front. It looks like dark days are coming our way. I'll do my best, but again no promises. Safe travels, ladies" Barb said as the signal disconnected.

# 19

## Warriors Are Home

THE LADIES ARRIVED at the medical center and made their way inside. Ellie held Sabina's hand as the electronic doors opened.

"Deep breaths, we can do this. Let's find Bill's room and go from there. One step at a time" Sabina said.

"Yes, one step at a time. We got this. No matter how bad it is, we will get through this together. Family, right?" Ellie said.

"Family. We got this," Sabina said.

They went to the information desk and were directed to Bill's room. The ladies stood outside the room for a few seconds and then made their way inside. Sabina walked in and first saw Rob laying on the bed. He smiled and pointed to the next bed near the window. Ellie stayed back giving Sabina time to be with Bill. Sabina opened the curtain and she found Bill sleeping facing the window. Sabina reached over and began caressing Bill's hair.

"Hey lady I have a girl and she has a bad temper" Bill said and began to laugh.

"William, William, do you still love me?" Sabina whispered to him.

"Forever and forever more. How about you Sunshine, do you still love me?" Bill answered.

"Forever and forever more. I am so glad you are home. I missed you so much" Sabina said.

Sabina reached over and kissed him. It was a passionate kiss that could be felt between both of their Spirits. Sabina then crawled into the bed with Bill and placed her body next to his, allowing her head to fall into his chest.

"I have no idea how we are going to do this. My heart was so empty while you were gone. The only truth I know is that I love you and I don't want to live without you" Sabina said.

"Sunshine you are my everything and I don't want us ever to be apart. This was a hard tour but Rob and I made it home. I know we worried you, and I am so sorry about that" Bill said.

"Bill, are you alright? I mean, I know you are in the hospital, but why are you here? I know my words are coming out all wrong. I don't know how to ask. I'm sorry. I am just so worried about you" Sabina said.

"I wish things would not have gone so wrong but we were ambushed. Do you want to hear this? Is it okay?" Bill asked.

"Bill, first I want to know how you are and then I will listen to the whole thing," Sabina said.

"Sunshine, I took a bad beating the last night we were there. I got pulled up from the well. I got dragged into a cave where there were new insurgents in the mix. One of them was very upset and kept calling me a killer. He decided to punish me for all the lives the Americans have taken. He strapped me to the wall and began to beat me with a cane. Like I said, I took a pretty bad beating; I can take a lot of pain but he concentrated on my spleen. Now the doctors are telling me that they might have to operate to remove it.. So they are pumping me with pain and anti-inflammatory meds. They want to wait a few days to see how my body responds to the treatment," Bill said.

"So we need to wait to see how your body responds?" Sabina inquired.

"Well my body is responding in a positive way to you being here Sunshine" Bill said with a little smile.

"Sunshine, things went very wrong when we were in the sandbox this last time. Rob and I were helping to relocate our troops from one side of town to the other. We assisted in providing additional security and escorts while the hummers were moving across the area. Rob and I held back to see if the tail gate was safe. The last Humvee was hit by an IED and then it caught on fire. Rob was struck in the leg when we were pulling soldiers out of the way. It was within a matter of seconds and we were surrounded by multiple insurgents. We were hooded and thrown into a truck and rode around for hours. When we stopped, we were at a village and they threw us in a dried up well" Bill then took a small break.

"Sunshine, the villagers did not have anything to do with us being kidnapped. They just did not know how to fight Al-Qaeda. They were in just as much trouble as we were in. It is amazing how easily people become fearful and manipulated. In a matter of a couple of nights the poor shepherds, farmers, women, and children, hardworking people, lost their peaceful living. They did not choose to be in that fight nor wanted to be part of it. When the leaders were not there they brought us food and water. The children would sneak candy and the women would throw us blankets to cover ourselves to protect us from the elements" Bill said.

"Rob was seriously hurt and from time to time the villagers would help me lift him so they could clean his wound. He would not have survived if not for their kindness. Honestly, Sunshine, I don't know if I would have made it through this awful time without these strangers. Every night that I could, I would climb out of the well and place the tracker from place to place.

I knew the military was trying to find us, but we were so deep the signal was weak. I would come back and check on Rob" Bill stopped and looked at Sabina.

"Are you still okay to hear this?" Bill asked.

"Of course, I am here for you. I can't do much to make you feel better but I can listen" Sabina replied.

"One evening after we heard the prayers end, a man came to the well. He pulled us both up and when I looked at him I saw the devil in his eyes. He took aim at Rob's leg and I made an effort to stop him. Then he turned on me and I was ready for him. He took a blade to my neck and started saying he was going to behead me. All he needed was your address so he could send you my head. He kept saying, "American tell me about your girl." I refused to speak so he took his rage out on my back. You have to forget everyone and just be a savage to survive. He beat me so badly I lost consciousness and then they threw us back into that hole.  For the next five days he did the same thing and he would end each night by saying, "American, tell me about your girl." The next day we heard helicopters over our heads and within a few hours we were rescued." Bill took a deep breath and began holding Sabina tighter.

"Bill, can I do anything to help you? You know I love you and I will always love you" Sabina said.

"Sunshine you are here and that is all I need. I just needed you to know because I want you in my life, but this is part of my life. I need to know that you are okay with all this. This is who I am and I know it's a lot to take in. I guess I don't want you to be surprised about this life" Bill insisted.

"Bill, look, I am a police officer. I get the tough life and tough choices. My career has brought me a different perspective on life. I get what you do and why you do it. You are a warrior and I commend you for your honor and valor. You don't have to explain anything further unless you want to talk about it. I am here for you and I will always be here for you. I love you and I always will. I don't want you to treat me like I am breakable. I'm a pretty strong person and I can handle anything" Sabina said.

"Listen Sunshine I don't question you or your love for me. I just know that love is fragile and I worry that our love might fall into the abyss" Bill said as he was fighting off his sleep. Sabina kissed him on his forehead and caressed him gently as she brushed away his hair. Bill soon fell asleep as he could not fight it anymore. Sabina waited for a few minutes and moved from the bed to the chair which was between the window and the bed. She waited a few more minutes to ensure Bill was in a deep sleep. Sabina then tip-toed outside of Bill's room and peaked into Rob's side. She could see that Ellis had made herself comfortable sitting next to Rob while holding his hand.

Sabina walked into the hallway and went to look for a nurse for an update and maybe a coffee or two. She walked into the nurse's station and attempted to get an update. The nurse was very kind but direct, when she informed Sabina that she was not family and therefore she could not provide much information. However, she told Sabina to wait for the doctor to do his rounds and she could ask him questions in front of Bill. She then guided Sabina to the cafeteria where she could get a few cups of coffee. Sabina came back with two cups of coffee and made her way back to her side of the room. Sabina resolved to the idea that she just had to sit tight and wait for the doctor to come around.

Sabina drank her coffee and waited for some news as she looked out the window. It was just a matter of time and she also fell asleep. A few hours later Sabina could feel someone shaking her awake. She woke up to a nurse telling her Bill's condition had not improved, in fact it was deteriorating each hour. Sabina was dazed and confused when Ellis sat next to her. The nurse tried to explain to her once more what was taking place and that they were quickly preparing Bill for surgery. The doctor came in and said,

"I know it is not the news you wanted to hear, but it looks like we caught it in time. We will have to remove Master Sergeant Young's spleen and make sure there is no infection. Barring any complications he should have a full recovery, but we need to move. We cannot afford to waste any more time so if you excuse me, I will come back with an update as soon as I possibly can." The doctor walked off as the medical staff pushed Bill's bed towards the door.

"Wait" Sabina yelled out, "can I kiss him goodbye" she asked.

"Of course," the nurse said.

Sabina kissed Bill gently on the forehead and then kissed him on his lips as she whispered, "William, William do you still love me?" As she pulled away from him, a tear rolled down her face.

"I am sorry Ma'am, but we have to go," the nurse said.

Ellis grabbed Sabina and pulled her back towards the window as they rolled Bill into surgery.

"Don't worry Sabina, Billie is strong, he will be fine" Ellis said.

"I just don't understand why he did not wake up. He was fine yesterday. I mean he looked fine to me" Sabina said as she was again holding back her tears.

Rob came back into the room too and quickly became confused. "Hey what is going on? Where is Bill?" he said.

"Surgery. They are taking his spleen out" Ellis said.

"Oh, I know they were talking about it. He really took a bad beating on the last day before we were rescued" Rob responded and then looked at Sabina "Oh, sorry we haven't met. You must be Bill's girl, the cop from Florida. I heard something or two about you. "

"Nice to meet you Rob. I am sorry, you were sleeping and I was too excited to stop and say hello." Sabina said.

"No worries, Bill was just as happy to see you. I think he might have waited for his surgery so he could see you. That is one hell of a guy" Rob said.

"Rob, what happened out there?" Ellis asked.

"I have known Bill for a while and we might have worked together a half dozen times. He normally works alone, which is mainly why he is so successful at what he does. Bill can walk into a bar, cave, or center of town to buy information and disappear before anyone notices him. I am not sure how he does it, but I am grateful there are guys like him. I received orders to relocate my unit and it had to be done expeditiously. Most of our troops were secured and all I needed to move were a handful of translators and a squad of friendlies we had been training. During the initial move we found no issues, but it was getting dark. That's when we got hit and we were hit hard. The last section had three vehicles and we were quickly blocked. We were sitting ducks. I only had one gunnery and one troop leader accompanying me. We were out-numbered and out-gunned. It was the perfect place for an attack; our communications could not be reached; it was a dark spot" Rob gathered his thoughts and continued.

"Men were shot from every direction, the trucks were blown away and I got shot in the leg. I was trying to find cover when parts of the truck came flying towards me. I thought I was a goner when I felt someone dragging me towards a building. I turned to fight and it was Bill who had come out of nowhere to help us, well, just me since everyone else perished in the fight. Bill told me that it was not a good day to die. He was carrying a duffle bag with cash money which he used to buy intel. I was shocked to see him throw the money into the fire and burn it up. If he was captured with the money he would have been immediately beheaded. There is a price of $5 million for the head of the Ghost. As the money went up in smoke, Bill tried to carry me when we were struck again by an IED. We went flying across the sand and soon were surrounded by insurgents. They hooded us, threw us in the back of a truck and drove for hours until we got to a village up the hills. Once there, they cut our patches off our uniforms and threw us into a deep dried-up well" Rob stopped and then looked at Sabina.

"Bill is a good guy and a strong guy. He will be fine. I tell you if it was not for him I would not be here." Ellis took his hand and helped him into his bed. "Ellie, you got a great brother. I know he loves you both. He would do all he could to keep up our spirits. He would sing songs, tell jokes, but the best part would be the stories he told me about both of you." Rob stopped.

"Why did you stop?" Ellis asked.

"I don't want to speak out of turn. I am sorry Sabina may I?" Rob said.

"Yes it will be nice to hear." Sabina said.

"Well some nights we did not see the insurgents, but when we did they would torment us. Bill took the brunt of it because he did not want them to kill me. The leader, we named him 'Woody', would come and ask us personal stuff. He would tell Bill, 'tell me about your girl' but Bill refused to answer anything. He would just look through him. Woody would become frustrated and torture him more. Later when we were alone, Bill would tell me that he did not want to speak about personal stuff so they could not fuck with his mind. Woody would lean into the well and whisper, 'tell me about your girl American.' Bill would never break, but I knew he was thinking about you.

We spent hours in that cave and Bill had the opportunity to escape. He would wait to make sure none of Woody's people were in the village. I am pretty sure the villagers were on our side and somehow they would signal it was clear. Bill would go out and place the tracking device in different locations to see if the signal was picked up. Every time he was gone I would pray for him to be safe and for him to be rescued. I did not want him to come back for me. It was a bad place. But Bill would always return and some nights he would bring extra food and water for me. I am alive because he refused to follow my orders and leave me behind and for that ladies, I will always be in his debt."

"Why don't you rest for a bit now?" Sabina said "we will wake you once they bring us some news."

Rob fell asleep as the two women sat and stared at the clock. A few hours later Sabina found herself once more standing in front of the doctor. "So the surgery went well. He is in recovery. Once we get the test results and make sure his blood levels are high enough, you will be able to see him." Sabina took a sigh of relief, but then panic struck. What if they don't let her into the ICU Unit since she was not family, she questioned?

"Oh, by the way Mrs. Young. Your husband told me to tell you he still loves you forever and forever more." The doctor said with a huge grin on his face as he winked and walked away.

"Damn that Bill" she said out loud, "He got the doctor on his side." She walked back into the room and shared the good news.

It was a matter of a few days later when the staff was wheeling Bill back into his room where Ellis, Rob, and Sabina were waiting for his return. The staff assured everyone that Bill was stable and he was just resting. There was no need to worry, but wait for him to wake up. Eight hours later, Bill became restless and woke to Sabina and Ellis eagerly watching for him to open his eyes.

"Hey strangers! How long was I out? "Bill asked as he was waking up.

"Billie, you were out for a while after your surgery. Good to see you alive, brother." Ellis kissed him on the cheek and then excused herself so Sabina and Bill could talk in peace.

"Sunshine, do you still love me?" Bill asked.

"Forever and forever more. How about you William? William, do you still love me?" Sabina responded.

"Forever and forever more. You know I do love you and I will always love you" Bill said.

"So what is next for us? I mean I know you are going to be here for a bit more, but can I help you when you go back to your home?" Sabina asked cautiously.

"Sunshine, my home will be wherever you want it to be. But the ranch in Wyoming will be your home if you want it to be. I would like to go back to the ranch if you are ready to get married" Bill said.

"I will go with you and marry you whenever you are ready. It does not have to be a big ceremony. I am good just going to the courthouse or anywhere" Sabina said.

"Pops talked to you about a traditional ceremony right? Patricia and I did not have a traditional ceremony. I never felt the calling for the ceremony until now. I am sure that we need to unite our Spirits in this life and the next. Like my parents and their parents for generations before. I know that I am asking you to believe in something you are not accustomed to, but I hope you understand" Bill pleaded.

"Bill, I did speak to your father about the ceremony and I will be honored to take part in your traditions. I can't wait for us to start our lives together" Sabina said.

Sabina and Bill spent time in the hospital as Bill was recovering. They would take long walks in the garden outside the hospital. Spending time with one another made it easy for them to settle into their new life. Bill was feeling better each day, and they would help Rob work on his rehabilitation. Rob wanted to get back to active duty, but there were complications with his recovery and the process was slow. Bill and Sabina kept encouraging him to work hard and stay strong. It was comforting to Bill to see how much Ellis had grown up and how she had taken an interest in Rob. Sabina and Bill watched as Ellis became closer to Rob and that he wanted to get to know Ellis. She was so kind and caring towards him. Ellis and Rob would talk for hours about their experiences and goals. This brought great joy and warmed their hearts.

As they walked through the garden and sat at the bench in front of the pond, Bill grabbed Sabina's hand and said "It looks like I will be heading home in a day or two."

"So it appears this is it" she replied in a somber tone.

Bill looked puzzled and focused on her expression. Sabina looked distant and stoic.

"I thought we had agreed that you were ready for the next step?" He paused, "But, if you are not, like I said before, I am willing to wait, Sunshine."

Sabina stood up and walked towards the pond. She looked at the koi who seemed to be as curious as Bill. Bill stood up and walked towards Sabina; he was unsure if she wanted him that close. He did not want to spook her away, but he did want to know what she was thinking about. The energy between them was too powerful and he embraced her by placing both his arms around her. Bill thought if they were going to part ways at least he could hold her once more.

"What are you talking about? We are not breaking up. Whatever gave you that idea? I am with you for the long haul. My silence is more like gratitude rather than hesitation. I was just waiting for you to be well enough to get our lives started" Sabina responded.

The doctors released Bill and explained that Rob would need to continue his rehabilitation for the next several months. They also received the news that because of his injuries Rob would not be allowed to return to active duty, and that he will be riding a desk for the remainder of his career. Rob and Ellis have hit it off well. They have been getting closer each day. Rob asked Bill if he could continue his rehabilitation with him at the ranch if he could get the doctors to agree to this new plan. It did not take long for the four of them to be heading to Wyoming with the hope of preparing for the wedding.

# 20

## Heading West

ONCE AT THE ranch, Ben greeted them with sage smoke to clear the air and dispel bad spirits. Ben had Bill's house ready for the couple and the additional cabin ready for the guest in order to separate the men from the women as tradition requires. Ben explained that each Native American tribe has different ways of celebrating weddings which are emotional events. Native American tribes are diverse in their practices and wedding traditions will vary between tribes. Certain tribes may use similar elements in their wedding ceremonies; they can also differ significantly. However, there are five Native American wedding traditions and rituals which transcend from tribe to tribe. Each wedding path requires baskets, blankets, fire, water, and a wedding base. Ben told Bill and Sabina the ritual preparations would begin in the morning or when they were ready to start. As called by tradition, the women and men needed to sleep in different locations. Bill and Rob stayed at the small cabin while the ladies remained in the main house. Ben of course had his own home and traveled between places making the preparations.

As the sun broke into the sky, Ben came over to Bill's cabin and snipped some locks of hair. Lucky that the Army had not given him a typical high top haircut so there were enough strands of his hair for the wedding braid. As Ben took hair from Bill, he marched it over while singing a traditional Cherokee hymn. The hair was gathered and Ellis helped Sabina braid it into her hair. The tradition according to Ben goes back centuries when a young warrior would leave hair for his bride on her pillow. The braiding symbolizes their unity on this earth and with their spirits. Once Sabina's long hair was braided, her body was to be washed in the hot springs. She had to ride up to the springs, disrobe and allow the healing waters to set all her fears free. Sabina was to return before sunset.

As the sun was sneaking away, Bill would ride to the hot springs and begin his ritual. This would be the only time the bride and groom would catch a glimpse of one another. They were not to speak or stop, however, as they were to exchange spots. As they passed one another, Bill would be able to brush Sabina's cheek with his hand. He planned on giving her a smile that warmed her heart and body.

Sabina woke up nervous and happy. She wished her parents were alive to see her happiness. It was not a feeling of sadness or sorrow; she simply could not find the words to explain this hollow feeling. Sabina was overjoyed, but something was missing from her big day. As she walked into the bedroom, she found Ellis preparing the five baskets.

"What is inside of them?" Sabina asked.

"Ben was very specific in his details. I have to place bread, water, sage, flowers, and rocks."

"Rocks?" Sabina asked.

"Well the bread and water is for you never to be hungry, the sage is to keep the bad spirits away. The flowers signify your joy and happiness. And the rocks are to guide your path. Rocks for Native Americans are used for many things: medicine wheels, to make a route, or designate areas. Rocks are part of the earth and the Creator made them to be protectors" Ellis laughed, "Look at me, I sound like Ben." The two started to laugh as Sabina noticed her beautiful gown laying across the bed. She walked towards it almost hesitating to touch it. It was lace with turquoise and orange embroidery around coral beads, creating an exquisite v-neckline.

As Sabina examined the Column silhouette design, she was captivated by the beads which had been delicately placed on the midline. As she touched the beads, Sabina could see that the design told a story of the land and its people. There were shapes of ridges, mountains, and valleys as well as the river and creeks. Sabina could also see the pattern of the stars and clouds. The back of the dress was designed to tell the story of the forced displacement of Indigenous people also known as the Trail of Tears. Each silver bead represented the 60,000 Indian members of the five tribes, Cherokee, Muscogee, Seminole, Chickasaw, and Choctaw that were forced to leave their ancestral homelands. They walked over thousands of miles and suffered from starvation, exposure to the elements, and countless diseases. About 15,000 died during the journey west prior to reaching their final destination: the government-appointed Indian Reservation also known as the "Rez." Sabina examined the delicate dress and she simply could not divert her eyes, she was mesmerized.

"That was Bill's mom's wedding dress. You are going to look beautiful in it. And once you are wed, new beads will be added so you and Bill will become part of the ritual for the next bride" Ellis told her.

"Oh Ellis, this is so beautiful I just cannot believe this is happening to me" Sabina said, "I just wished my parents were here with me to enjoy all of this. I just cannot explain it. All I can say is that I miss them terribly."

"I know what you mean. I miss mine as well. I have no words to thank Bill and Ben for taking me in. And I hope you and I will soon be like sisters" Ellis replied.

"Oh, Ellis, you are my sister," Sabina said.

They were gathering the last few items for the baskets when they heard someone riding a motorcycle on the ranch. Then they heard a knocking at the door. "Who could that be? Bill cannot see you before the wedding, it's tradition. I will bet the guys are messing around with a motorcycle outside" Ellis responded as she walked to the door to open it.

"Can I help you?" Ellis said as a short woman stood in the doorway holding a helmet in one hand and a large package on the other.

"Sure Doll, you can show me to the bride-to-be. I came to make sure she did not get cold feet. Tell her I brought her socks" Barb said as she pushed her way through the doorway.

"Barb? What are you doing here?" Sabina said as she peaked out of the bedroom.

"Doll, I came for the party. I heard there were going to be Cowboys and sexy Indians running around. I am hoping to snag a half-naked fellow for myself. What? I still got it!" Barb said as she put her hand on her hips and walked around like a runway model. "So tell me Doll where is your Ghost? You guys left the medical center and thought I would not know you were getting married?" Barb questioned.

"Oh God, Barb, did you not get my text messages? I know we did not make wedding invitations, but you are family. You know you are family right?" Sabina said.

"I am just giving you grief girl. Come here let me look at you. You are going to make a beautiful bride. Plus, this gave me an opportunity to run my Harley up here. Wow, the view is amazing" Barb said as she hugged Sabina.

"I brought gifts for the bride. I got your white boots for the wedding. Since you are not Cherokee you are not allowed to wear the traditional moccasins. So I researched it and with a little help from my new pen pal Ben, I found you white boots. I had them stitched with your and Bills' initials in the lining along with your special day. The boots are the mother of the bride's gift. I know I am not your Mom, but I am sure you are missing her more than ever today." Sabina could not help herself and began hugging Barb.

"I am not sure what I would have done without you, Barb. You are one hell of a woman. Of course, I would be honored if you stand with me during the ceremony" Sabina responded. "Well, let's not stand around, put me to work. I am sure you will not be able to stand after the wedding night" Barb said as they all began to laugh.

"Come on Barb" Ellis said, "You can help me fix up the honeymoon cabin. It's about ten miles on the west side of the property. We can either ride a horse, take the ATV, or you can give a ride. It is up to you" Ellis continued.

"Hop on girl. I will take you up there on my beast" Barb said.

"We will be back in a couple of hours. You will need to stay inside of the house and rest. Remember, no peeking at Bill, it's bad luck" Ellis warned her as she and Barb rode away.

In a matter of twenty minutes, Barb and Ellis arrived at the honeymoon cabin to make the last few preparations. The cabin was small but perfect for the honeymoon suite, one room along with a fireplace, a kitchenette, bathroom, and a wrap-around porch. The first floor had little furniture, just a small table with chairs, a couch, a loveseat, and a chair. It also has a second floor with a large bed that overlooks the mountain and the creek making the place perfect for the two lovers. Barb and Ellis placed fresh flowers around the house,  made the bed, added firewood, and decorated the front porch. The last touches to make the place perfect was to replenish the pantry and decorate the front door with the feather wreath which was blessed with sage smoke.

"Doll, do we have to do anything else?" Barb asked as she took one last look.

"Well, we have to wait for Ben. He will be here shortly with the blanket for the wedding night. I don't know all of the details, he said it had to be prepared and we just had to make sure the bedding was white. Once the blanket is ready we will lay it over and it will bless the couple during their wedding night."

As the ladies were sitting outside on the porch, they saw a rider coming across the prairie. They could see the lonesome rider coming closer, and even from a distance Ellis could see it was Ben.

"Hey Barb, have you met Ben? He is Bill's father and he is riding up here with the blessed blanket. He will be so happy to finally meet you in person." Ellis said.

"Wow, that is one tall drink of water" Barb said as she tried to tidy herself up.

As the rider approached, Ben stood tall in his saddle as he commanded the moment. Ben stopped in front of the ladies, and dismounted from his horse with the blanket. Ben started the sage blessing with smoke clearing his path. Ben came up the stairs with the blanket and approached Barb and Ellis.

"Good evening, ladies. I got the blanket ready for the bed. I will need to place it on the bed upstairs and then I will be more than happy to sit and visit with everyone." Ben walked upstairs and placed the blanket over the bed. He said a blessing for the couple and then proceeded downstairs and met with them..

"What is the blanket about? I mean, what is the deal? I mean, what is the tradition surrounding the blanket?" Barb asked Ben.

Ben sat on the porch swing next to Barb as he began to explain the tradition. "It is important for the couple to be joined in both body and spirit. The blessed blanket will be taken to the ceremonial grounds. The couple will be blessed with holy feathers of an eagle as they stand on the healing circle made with rocks. Before they drink from the water base, they will be wrapped with the blanket. This symbolizes their union on this earth, once Billie and Sabina drink at the same time out of the water base, their union will be spiritual," Ben explained as he walked closer and closer until he was standing next to Barb. They stood together for a few minutes in silence, but Barb could feel Ben's energy and she too found her spirit drifting during the romantic scene. Barb was so attracted to Ben that she could have sworn he could feel her heart beat faster and faster as he came closer to her.

The night was beautiful; a full moon and the stars twinkling above the entire valley. The place looked almost like a sketch in a storybook as the wind blew lightly over them. Barb had to step away from Ben or she felt like she would lose all control, so she walked to the railing,

"Who is that rider in the distance?" she asked as Ellis walked towards her. Barb felt a quick gasp of wind that gave her a shiver. She rubbed her hands on her arms as if to warm herself up.

Ben then took the opportunity to grab the small blanket from the swing and wrap Barb with it. "The night air can be deceiving at times especially during this time of the year." He gently placed the blanket and wrapped it around Barb, but also held her for a few seconds.

Barb smiled at Ben as she whispered, "Thank you."

"Oh, that should be Sabina. She is going to the creek where the Moon kisses the water. She will take her final cleansing before the wedding. Sabina will bathe under the moonlight and then cover herself with a white gown. She will wrap herself with a blanket and ride back to the cabin." A few minutes later they could see Sabina riding back; she will cross paths with Bill going the opposite way. "Billie will be heading to the creek for his final cleansing. As the riders cross paths, they cannot stop or talk to one another. They are only allowed to look at their future mate and keep moving forward. If you want to see the riders meet, look over the ridge just to your right and you should be able to see them."

Both Barb and Ellis could not hold their excitement for Bill and Sabina. They stood perfectly still as they could see Sabina riding Peanut back from the creek wearing a white gown and covering herself with a blanket. Sabina's body was sparkling in the moonlight as it reflected on the drops of water that covered her exposed skin. They could see Bill approaching wearing just blue jeans and was only covered with a blanket. He slowly approached Sabina; the two of them were riding close to one another. What they could not catch was that as Bill passed Sabina he gently reached over and caressed her hair and down her arm. He also gave her that killer smile that warmed her heart. Sabina felt her heart skip a beat or two as Bill was looking at her. Sabina understood the sum of the traditions and culture, but at that moment she did all she could to contain herself from reaching over and grabbing Bill. Sabina pulled herself back and did not fall for that temptation.

As Bill got closer to Sabina, he reached over and touched her hair. He caressed her face gently and brushed her long brown hair and arm. He wanted to stop and hold Sabina while helping her dismount off Peanut. He could imagine them both kissing until they laid on the ground and used their blankets for warmth. Bill wanted to take her and make her his once more while they glittered in the moonlight. Bill felt his love leaping out of his heart and body. He could feel the energy between the two of them, Bill knew that all he had to do was to stop his horse and all his dreams would come true. Bill's mind was thinking about the passionate kissing they would share that night, among other things. His body was aching for hers, and it would be so simple just to break tradition and simply reach for her.

Bill had strong temptation at his side and it took all his strength of character to fight off the demons luring him to take Sabina. Bill took a deep long breath and pushed off all his passion and animalistic hunger for her. Bill stood tall and pushed through to the creek as Sabina kept riding on to their future home. Once at the creek, Bill dismounted his horse and threw himself into the cold water. He knew he needed to clear his head and cool off his body from the lusting temptation he had just experienced. The cold water covered his entire body and cleansed him from head to toe.

Calling on the Creator to guide him and give him strength to wait for his bride, Bill imagined the number of warriors who had to fight off their natural instinct and not take their brides early. Bill needed to be strong and remember his bloodline and the promise he made to honor his people. Bill laid in the moonlight floating over the waters as it reflected like a mirror. He could almost feel the warmth of the earth as his mind refocused on the day ahead. Bill finally stood up and thanked the Creator for giving him the gifts he had received during his lifetime. Accounting for his family and blessings was an important part of Bill's ritual. Soon the moon would be hidden and it would be his wedding day. Finally, he and Sabina would be together and bound by eternity.

# 21

## The Wedding Ritual

THE MORNING OF the wedding Bill got up early and saddled his horse. He took his morning ride along with a nice cup of coffee. He thought about dropping one off at Sabina's cabin for her to have before the rush of the day. However, Bill did not want to take chances of them seeing one another. So he decided not to press the issue and to take the route far away from her as he could not be seen by anyone. Bill took a path that circled the mountain range. He climbed to the top of the ridge as he drank his coffee. He enjoyed the breeze and brisk chill in the air. Bill wanted to take a moment just to reflect on his life and all the possibilities of his future with Sabina. Bill was content and grateful for all the good things he was experiencing. He took a deep breath and realized that life had not been easy, but that he was finally in a good place. Bill finished his coffee and went back down to meet his bride.

The setting for the wedding was ready. The clearing was prepared and a medicine circle was set for the bride and groom to make their way to one another. At the center of the medicine circle was a small table wrapped in white linen. On top of the table stood a lone ceramic Native American wedding vase. The vase is handcrafted with two drinking spouts which are connected by a single vase filled with water. The wedding vase symbolizes the union between two separate lives and as they drink together, those lives come together as one. The vase was painted to represent the Cherokee Nation and it had one tear drop crystal at its center. The bride and groom approach the medicine circle together as the high priest blessed them with an eagle feather and sage smoke.

The time came for the bride and groom to join the guests and take their sacred vows. The guests had come from the Rez and the nearby town. Sabina had Barb and Ellis standing with her. Bill asked Rob to be his best man. The ceremony began with traditional Native American sounds of drums and chants. Bill and Sabina approached the circle from opposite sides of the clearing and stood still before entering the medicine circle. As they stood perfectly still Bill admired Sabina's beauty.  She stood stoic in her white gown which sparkled in the rays of sunshine. He was thinking of her strength and passion. He could not believe how blessed he was at this very moment. Bill knew nothing would ever be as beautiful as his soon-to-wife, Sabina.

At the same time, Sabina could not believe she was holding herself together. She had never in her life been so nervous. She was no longer scared or frightened; she in fact was so content and had to do all she could not to run into Bill's arms. She wanted him forever and forever. Her heart was pounding so loud that she believed it would over-power the sound of the drums and chants. "Calm down" she told herself, and with a glance at him with that killer smile, she found her spirit no longer drifting.

Sabina was ready for this leap of faith and she knew there was nothing more that she wanted but to be with Bill forever. She looked at him and saw the majestic man that was going to keep her safe, happy, and be her heaven-on-earth.  Bill stood tall, strong, and sexy with his tight jeans and white shirt tucked in as if it were tailor-made. Simple. His broad shoulders and muscular body were all she wanted and there was nothing else she would ever need.

As they made their way to the center of the circle, they were bathed with sage smoke. Each individual path represented their own story and the way in which it led to their union. The road was rough and made them stumble along the way. However, each step, no matter how difficult, would lead them to one another. The end of the path represents the moment where their spirits will unite for eternity.

They stepped into the center as the Medicine Man who blessed them and the well of water inside the vase. Not many words were spoken, the couple did not exchange vows, but when instructed, they drank out of the water vase together. The Medicine Man then had the couple turn and face west and then east. He then introduced them as husband and wife both in the Spirit world as well as on Mother Earth.

As tradition calls, unlike other cultures after the wedding ceremony, there is a wedding reception for the guests only. The newlyweds do not attend. Bill and Sabina simply ride off into the sunset together wrapped in their ceremonial blanket in order to consummate their marriage in the wedding bed. Bill lifted Sabina and placed her on his horse then jumped on and cradled her in his lap.

Bill took his time galloping slowly and kept her wrapped with their blanket. As the horse's body moved, so did Sabina and Bill. Her hips lightly brushed over his powerful manhood crashing into him like the waves on the coast. Every time they moved Sabina got closer and closer to Bill's body. Bill thought Sabina's lips were begging to be kissed by more than the light. The friction was so intense that it excited them both.  Sabina leaned into Bill and they began to kiss and caress one another.

They took the small path which led them to their wedding cabin. Not all traditions were lost, however, once at the cabin Bill helped Sabina off the horse and lifted her over the door's threshold. Sabina held on to Bill as he lifted her and carried her into their wedding cabin. He took her up the stairs and began kissing her as he lay her on the wedding blanket. He took his time kissing her neckline and chest as he began to slip off her dress.

He gently placed it over the back of the chair inside of the room. He took the time to remove his shirt exposing his muscular chest. When he turned Bill could see Sabina was wearing some type of corset that hugged her body. He walked back to her slowly. He did not know how to get Sabina's body out of the corset, but he knew he would have a great time figuring it out. He knelt down and began by removing her white cowgirl boots. He placed them aside and started stroking her legs upwards. He began by kissing each inch of her exposed skin. Quickly Bill discovered the hidden zipper in the back of the garment. As Sabina's body became bare, he noticed Sabina had started taking her braids out and now her long brown hair flowed freely over her body. Bill stopped for a second and caught his breath because it would be the first time they would make love as husband and wife. Bill wanted to place his lips on every inch of Sabina's body.

"William, William, do you still love me?" Sabina whispered into Bill's ear.

"Sunshine, I will love you forever and forever more. We are now bound by body and spirit. I am yours and you are mine till the end of time. But I want more from you than you can imagine. I want your love, heart and your soul. You got my everything and I don't ever want you to doubt my love."

Bill fully undressed and moved to the bed and laid next to his wife. He reached for her and helped straddle her body over his exposed manhood. Sabina leaned down to kiss Bill as he placed his hands on the small curve of her back. Sabina took full advantage of the moment and they became one. She began rocking back and forth and kissed Bill as their flow and rhythm got its groove. As each wave of pleasure overtook Sabina, she also felt Bill's manhood erupt. How she wanted him to be inside her, how she wanted him to explore every single inch of her soul, all that she always hid inside of her heart, body and soul. Bill let out a warrior moan as they climaxed together again. Sabina's body dropped on top of Bill. They needed some rest but continued to make love because they craved one another.

Bill held Sabina and then came up with the strength to say, "I love you. I know what makes you happy, and what scares you, but I want you to tell me what makes you sad. Talk to me. I want you to talk to me. I want to know what makes you sad, because I never want you to suffer. Not while I'm around. I never want you to feel lonely, or hurt ever again. I promise you Sunshine; nothing will ever keep me from making it home to you. You are my heart" Bill said as he gave her another long, deep passionate kiss.

Sabina found herself falling deeper and deeper in love for Bill. She could not believe that she had found the perfect person for her. She recalled her mother's words telling her that if she waited for love, it would find her. "Don't worry. Everyone has their person, the one they are meant to be with for the rest of their lives. The problem is that we get scared to be alone so we rush to the wrong one. Don't run to the wrong guy Chiquita, when the right one is two steps behind you" she would tell Sabina over and over.

Sabina smiled at her mother's words while she watched Bill napping after their love-making. He looked so peaceful and content. He had fallen asleep in her arms while she softly ran her fingers through his hair. She imagined their beautiful days on the ranch taking long walks, talking about everything or nothing and simply enjoying one another. Sabina began making plans for them to enjoy time at the ranch and then maybe later on in the year travel to Florida to check on her property. Sabina was so grateful to be here in Bill's arms and heart. She could not imagine being anywhere else and she knew finally what it meant to be truly happy.

The days together came and went. They were settling into a routine around the house and the ranch. They were both so happy holding one another each night and working the ranch

during daylight. Bill took it upon himself to teach Sabina about taming horses and taking care
of the land. With her green thumb, they started making plans for her garden and happily caring
for some of the horses that had been rescued in the area. With each day's passing, their bond
drew even closer as they kept their loving promises to one another.

# 22

## Keep the Home Fires Burning

AS THE WINTER entered spring and the spring to summer, Bill began receiving calls
from Gaby. He did not want to return to action, but he had one more mission to complete. It
was sad news and he had a difficult time coming to grips with the reality that he had to leave
Sabina once more. After taking a long ride into the prairie, he made his way back to their cabin
where he found Sabina sitting on the porch looking at her cellphone. Tears were rolling down
her face as he approached her.

"I guess the honeymoon has ended. I just got a call from the Sheriff. I need to report
back as soon as possible. I am needed in Florida. The whole country has lost its mind and I
need to help with the civil unrest taking place in the county. I am so sorry, but I cannot say no. I
have a duty to them but I don't want to leave you" Sabina cried.

"Sunshine, I got a text from Gaby. I am being called in as soon as possible, too. I have
to go get a few guys out of Baghdad. I guess this means we are both deploying. I am so sorry
about your county. What can I do to help you prepare?" Bill said as he knelt next to her.

"Bill, I am scared for us. I don't want to be away from you. Not today, not ever. This is so unfair. Why do we have to be called in? Why can't they just let us be happy? Why can't we just say no and quit? "Sabina said angrily.

"Why don't we do this? You go to Florida and I will do my thing and then we will call it quits. You know neither one of us wants to go, but we have an obligation. So Sunshine, while we are apart for a bit, promise that we will be in each other's heart and soul? Promise to keep me in your heart forever. It is just one moment in our story; it will not be forever, I promise." Bill said gently as he helped Sabina to her feet.

"William, you asked me what makes me sad. This is what makes me sad. William, do you still love me?" Sabina whispered as she fell into his arms.

"Forever and forever more. Sunshine, do you still love me?" he replied.

"Forever and forever more"

"Then we are good. Just keep me in your heart. Now we got to shake off our fears since we got company coming for the bonfire. Rob and Ellie should be here soon. Pops already got the firewood ready.  Come on, we still have time together, let's not waste it being sad." Bill said as they walked inside to prepare for their friends and subsequent mission.

That last evening Bill and Ben decided to have a beautiful bonfire to send everyone off and on their way. Ben invited Ellis, Rob, and Barb back to the ranch, but Barb could not make the trip. Ben had learned that Ellis and Rob had received orders to report to their bases as well, and he wanted to send them off with a sage blessing.  Bill explained to Ben the news regarding him and Sabina both being called to duty and having to report immediately for another mission. Ben was not surprised and told Bill to stay the course and that the Creator would watch over everyone. After a nice dinner, they all sat outside enjoying the stars, the weather, and one another.

"So brother, did you get your orders too?" Rob asked Bill as he began pulling out his guitar from the case.

"Yes, I meant to talk to you about that. I got my orders to hook up with a unit at Fort Bragg. From there we are deploying to the sandbox to assist in a rescue mission" Bill responded.

Rob continued and said "The doctors told me I will never be back in action, but the Army found me a nice cozy desk to ride. I don't know, my brother. I am not sure how I can lead a command from an office. It doesn't sound like I should be in a nice office while guys like you are eating dirt."

"You are kidding me right? You got a desk job and you are complaining? Look Rob, I am not sure how to tell you this but you of all people should count your blessings. You survived that snake pit of a well we were thrown in for a reason. I am not sure what the Creator has in store for you, but getting killed on the other side of the world is not it. Be grateful and enjoy your gift."

"Well, I am glad you are in such a great mood brother, because I need to talk to you about something else," Rob said.

"Before you ruin my day I need to ask you for a favor, since the girls are inside grabbing our drinks. Will you take care of my family if anything happens to me in the sandbox? I know I got my father, but now I got my wife and sister to think about. I need to know they will be taken care of if I cannot find my way home. So brother, will you take care of my family in my absence?"

Rob could not hold back his emotions and he gave Bill a hug. "It would be an honor my brother, but you always make it home. I know we got to take care of business before we deploy, but now you got everything to come home to. I also need to ask you for a favor. I need your blessing. I know you have seen how close Ellie and I have become. I am not sure if my head would be straight without her. Now I can't imagine living one day without her. I want what you have with your American girl.  Bill I am very serious. Without her I am not sure if I would have made it through those dark days of recovery. It might take me a lifetime, but all I want is to make Ellie happy.  Can I count on your blessing?"

Bill looked at Rob and said with a sternness in his tone, "You know I promised Scott to take care of her. After her last romantic experience, Ellie has been timid about giving her heart away. Before I answer you I need to know, is this just you or does she know you love her? Have you told her how you feel? Does she know what she is getting into? Do you? I am not about to give my little sister's heart away without you knowing who she is."

"Bill I promise you I would not be asking if Ellie was not in agreement first. She loves and respects you like an older brother and her keeper. All I can tell you is what I told her. I promise to make sure she knows she is loved every day. I promise to make sure that she is never scared, alone or lonely. She has my heart and if Ellie ever needs me to walk away I will, but she will always be my first priority."

"Well Rob, then all I can say is welcome to the family. We are one messed up group who love one another unconditionally. You both have my blessing" Bill shouted.

"Bill I know that I do not need to ask you but I need to also take care of home affairs. You and I have been through the devil's belly and back. I need to know you will always take care of my Ellie. I need to hear you say it brother, now that we are being deployed. If I don't

make it back, will you keep my love safe?"

"Rob, I know it's tradition and part of the deployment plan. Of course you can always

count on me. Always."

As the men were talking, Ellie and Sabina sat on the porch waiting for the right time to

join them. Sabina took a long deep breath to find the strength to get through the night.

"What is wrong Sabina, you look so sad?" Ellie asked.

"I am sure Bill is telling Rob about our orders to return to the real world. I just got a bad

feeling about this one. I am not sure why, but it all seems so rushed. I just thought we would

have more time together. We just found one another and now.." Sabina protested.

"It's okay to feel that way. You are new to this type of lifestyle. Don't get me wrong;

you have a dangerous career, but you are used to being able to return home every day. The

military is different: when we get deployed, home is not around the corner. Once we settle into

our civilian lives, boom, we are re-deploying. It's a bit of a vicious cycle like the Mad Hatter's

merry-go-'round.  You feel what you feel and it is all good. I got you. You are not alone" Ellie

said.

"Oh, Ellie I am so sorry, I know you are deploying as well. Where are you headed? Are

you going back to sea?" Sabina asked as she tried to pull back her tears.

"No, I am an idiot. About a year or so ago I asked to be reassigned to a combat unit. I

thought I was a Bad Ass. I could lead a convoy behind enemy lines. Well, I got my wish and

now I am also headed to the sandpits with the boys. Oh, Sabina, why did I do that? I am not worried about me, I am worried that the guys are going to be worried that I am there. Why am I so hardheaded?" Ellis said, holding back her own tears.

"What is going on Ellie? You never gave the impression that you are not together? What is really on your mind? You know the guys are strong" Sabina was puzzled by Ellie's response.

"Sabina, I am not sure if you know, but Rob and me? Well Rob and I are together. I thought I was just helping him recover, but soon we were together. He loves me like I have never been loved in my life. He cares for me deeply and I cannot imagine my life without him. I guess it's like you and Bill. Rob is my soulmate much like Bill is yours. What can I do to make sure he does not worry about me?" Ellis pleaded.

"Oh girl, you got it bad. I guess you two will be getting married soon."

"He is asking Bill right now. I thought while we were deployed you might have time to help me plan the wedding. I know it's presumptuous of me, but you are really all the family I got" Ellie said.

"Absolutely my dear. What do you think about a beach wedding? I can plan it while I am waiting for Bill to return. I am heading back to Florida, and I am sure I can get inspired while I am there. What do you think?" Sabina said with a big smile on her face.

"Sabina, I always wanted a sister. I am so glad you are mine"

"Me too. Me too. Now let's go see what our men are up to." They started to walk towards the guys when Sabina yelled "Who brought their guitar?"

"My future brother-in-law, Rob, will be the entertainment tonight" Bill said with his killer smile.

Rob sat down and began strumming his guitar and said, "Any requests?" And before anyone responded he started to sing,

"Shadows are fallin' and I'm runnin' out of breath

Keep me in your heart for a while

If I leave you it doesn't mean I love you any less

Keep me in your heart for a while" Rob then stopped as he noticed everyone listening intently. "Was that a bad selection? " Rob questioned.

"No, brother, I think it is perfect for the occasion," Bill said.

They spent the rest of the night singing songs, telling stories, and jokes. They laughed, they cried and made good memories to hold onto in the days to come.

# 23

## The Last Mission

WHEN MORNING CAME, Bill and Sabina found themselves driving away from their precious ranch. Rob and Ellis had made other arrangements for themselves. They were heading to the airport where Bill would head to an undisclosed military base and Sabina to Tampa, Florida.  As they approached the terminal, Sabina began to sob, she could feel something was wrong. She turned to Bill and said, "I love you William. I will always love you, my William."

Bill stopped dead in his tracks, and dropped his bag so he could grab Sabina and hold her tight, "We are tied together. You just need to keep the fires lit and I will be right next to you. You just need to keep me in your heart for a while. I promise you it will just be for a little while. Trust me, we are together, we will always be together even if we have an ocean between us. We are one. I love you forever and forever more." Bill kissed Sabina with a passionate kiss that made people stop and stare. He did not care, he just simply loved her and he knew she loved him.

Bill watched Sabina walk to her boarding area. He was hoping she would turn around one last time. "Come on Sunshine, please turn around one more time. Come on baby, please turn around. I need to see you once more. Come on" Bill pleaded to God. She seemed so far away. When Sabina finally turned around, Bill was standing in the same place where they embraced. Sabina felt her heart break, but she had to be brave and push on. Her mission was clear: go to Florida to help and make it home to her Bill. Sabina worried about Bill. Every deployment seems to be more and more dangerous. She could not keep from worrying, but she told herself to keep it together because she wanted him to be strong. Sabina blew Bill a kiss as he gave her that killer smile one last time before she boarded. Sabina then placed her hand over her heart as she whispered, "William, William I love you forever and forever more." Bill took a deep breath as he also placed his hand over his heart as he murmured to Sabina, "Forever and forever more. Keep me in your heart. I love you."

Bill stood still until Sabina disappeared into the security screening crowd. He prayed for her safety and he wanted to run to her and hold her one more time. Bill pulled together all his strength and walked towards his gate. He was heading to South Carolina where he was to join his unit and make his way to Germany. From Germany, he would be deployed to the Middle East, where exactly, he was not sure. But the mission was going to be a difficult one because American soldiers were trapped behind enemy lines and they were scheduled to be beheaded. Sabina reached her destination in a matter of hours while Bill's travels took days. They each had to do their parts separately, although their hearts were one. This commitment unfortunately called for them to be apart.

# 24

## The Cost of Freedom

DOCTOR SULLY GOT to the room and he was met with a team member yelling "she is bleeding out." "Why is she not in surgery?" Sully questioned.

Someone yelled out, "She was too weak. We were pumping her with fluids and I thought she was stable. Then her blood pressure dropped. I called for the code and I did not know what else to do. Sully looked in horror as the blood began to flow over onto the floor. Then all of a sudden the officer's cell phone rang from inside of Sully's pocket. He quickly stepped out of the room to answer as Dr. Smith walked into the room.

He prayed to all that was holy that it was William. "Hello, this is Dr. Sullivan, is this William?" Again, a long pause occurred as if the words uttered were traveling across space. Static, and more static. Sully knew someone was on the other line but he could not make out the words. "William, William, Bill, is this Bill?" he yelled but the call disconnected.

Sully turned to see two police officers walking towards him. They approached and said, "Doctor, I am so sorry it took us a while to identify the deputy. She is Sabina Contreras Goodwin, a Reserve Deputy Sheriff. It took us a bit to figure it out because of the riots and she recently updated her name. I guess she got married so she is now Young. How is Deputy Young doing? Is she going to make it?" Sully was furious at their attitude when he heard them say, "Her Sheriff is a pistol. He is going to be pissed off because we didn't ID her sooner."

Sully walked into her room and held her hand as she was struggling to catch her breath. Dr. Smith was doing everything to save her life. Sully leaned over and heard her say, "William, William."

Sully held her hand and whispered, "I am here you are not alone, Sabina." The phone rang once more and Sully picked up quickly and asked, "William, William are you there? I am here with your wife, Sabina."

"No, Doctor, it is Commander Robert Stevens. I am not sure how to tell you that Master Sergeant William Young was shot in the line of duty."

Sully let go of Sabina's hand and walked out of the room. As he made it to the hallway he could hear Smith say "time of death 2359."

"Commander, I am sorry to say that Master Sergeant William Young's wife Deputy Sheriff Sabina Contreras Goodwin Young was shot in line of duty as well. All extraordinary efforts were taken to save her life, however, her injuries were massive and we lost her" Sully replied.

After a long pause, Rob said "Doctor, excuse me but, do you know what time Sabina was shot?"

Sully was puzzled by the question but he said, "She was brought in around 8:00 P.M. but transport was diverted. So if I had to guess it was around 7:15 P.M. or 1915 hours."

"Bill was my best friend, and he was involved in a very dangerous mission. He paid off the insurgents for the freedom of several American soldiers who were scheduled to be beheaded. We got word that they had been freed but it was a set-up. Bill AKA The Ghost was a marked man. There was a price for his head of over $5 million. Once he left the rendezvous, he was followed and he was struck by a sniper. Bill was shot at 1215 hours, the exact time Sabina was shot stateside. I guess the Creator had other plans for them.  We managed to pull him out of the dusty street and transported him to a MASH Unit nearby.  Bill's thoughts were only on his true love Sabina till his last breath." 'Tell my Sunshine I must be the luckiest man alive because she was my joy. I might not get to Heaven but I have walked with an angel since the day we met. Promise me you will tell her I will be waiting for her. Sabina, you are my everything forever and forever more.' Doctor, Master Sergeant William Michael Young died in the line of duty serving our country. I just received the notice that he did not make it a few minutes ago."

"My God, Commander, I cannot believe what you are telling me. How is it possible that they were both shot at the same time? That they both died a few minutes apart?  What are the odds of that happening? Oh Lord, I am so sorry for your loss" Sully said while still trying to wrap his head around the news.

"Love is more precious than gold Sir, and too many people take that for granted."  After a long pause Rob said, "Doctor, the United States Military thanks you for all you have done as well as the staff in order to help save the life of fallen Deputy Sheriff Sabina Young. I will need to secure a flight and bring Master Sergeant Young's body stateside. I will reach out to the local Sheriff for Sabina's remains to be taken to their final resting place in Wyoming. Once again thank you for all your kindness" Rob said.

"Commander, I know this seems like the most inappropriate request, but I would like to join you when they are laid to rest. It would be a great honor to be able to assist in their service" Sully implored.

"Yes, of course Sir. I will reach out to you once we have made all the notifications and arrangements" Rob responded.

"I look forward to your call and God Bless You" Sully said before the call disconnected.

Sully said his final goodbye to Sabina realizing her fighting spirit no longer was among the living.  He then grabbed his gear and headed home. As he made his way out of the hospital, Sully's attention was disrupted by an ocean of red and blue lights. Sully could not believe the number of officers arriving at the hospital. The first SUV parked and out came the Sheriff quickly followed by two officers dressed in their Honor Guard Gear, campaign hats, white shirts, black trousers, and shiny shoes. He heard the Sheriff bark orders to the two police officers as he led his deputies inside through the ambulance bay.

The sheriff was greeted by Dr. Smith, who shared the bad news that Sabina had passed. Holding his tears back, the Sheriff exclaimed "We are here and she will no longer be alone." Sully watched as the two Honor Guard Deputies took their place in front of Sabina's door guarding and keeping her company. The additional officer's lined up at attention at the ambulance bay waiting to escort her back to their station.

It was then that Sully realized he still had Sabina's cell phone in his pocket. "I will take it to Wyoming once I get the Commander's call." Sully sat quietly inside his car contemplating the events of the day. He then reached for the ignition and the radio station started playing Keith Urban's version of **To Love Somebody**. Sully listened to the lyrics of the song as he made his way home when a particular lyric caught his attention.  Sully immediately pulled over to hear Urban sing, 'If I ain't you, ain't got you' Sully placed his hands over his face and said, "I get it, Sabina, you could not live without your William and he could not live without you. Not on this earth, not ever. Lord, why is love so fragile?"

# Author's Note

Dear Readers,

Thank you so much for joining us in this journey. Below you will find a sample of the next generation. We hope you enjoy what happens next in **Love Can Be Deceiving.**

# 1     Ellis Francis Walker

ELLIS FRANCIS WALKER could not believe she was standing in Afghanistan ready to lead her squad into the city. First Lieutenant E. F. Walker, one of the first females to lead a platoon during war time in a battlefield. Ellie needed to calm her nerves before they got the best of her. It was her first time taking point and she was ready for her mission. Ellie wanted to prove she was capable of this operation, and this particular mission was essential. She tried to catch some sleep, but her mind kept taking her to the other side of the world wrapped up in Rob's arms.  It seemed like a million years ago when they were last together, but it was only two weeks prior. Ellie looked at the clock and thought, "hell, why fight my memories. Maybe this is what my mind needs to relax." Finally she surrendered and allowed her mind to drift towards Rob.

Ellie thought of the days prior to their deployment; she and Rob found themselves hiking near the Red Rock Ridge in Utah. Rob knew it was Ellie's first deployment to the desert and he so wanted her to have good memories to hang on to. "Come on Ellie we can reach the top of the ridge and from there you can see the entire valley," he said as he held her hand. Ellie thought he was crazy for dragging her on a two-mile hike days before they were to be separated, however once they reached the top, all she could see was the beautiful blue sky and green grass.

"Rob, it looks like the sky and the earth are kissing," she said with excitement.

"This is my favorite place on the entire planet. I have been around the world a couple of times, but for me this place is magical," he replied.

"Rob, how did you find this place? It is breathtaking, and it is beautiful," Ellie said as she took a step closer to the edge of the cliff.

Rob grabbed her and pulled her back towards him saying, "Ellie careful, one missed step and this place becomes deadly. No worries, I got you, I got you. I will always take care of you." Ellie turned and found herself facing Rob, "I know you are a good man, Robert Stevens. I trust you. I know you got my back" she said.

Rob could not help himself and he began to kiss Ellie. Rob knew she was the girl for him, the girl of his dreams, and he wanted Ellie to know how much he loved her. She had never felt this type of love or passion before. She had relationships in the past, but this one was different; this was true love. Ellie was ready to give herself to Rob; mind, body and soul. Rob pulled away from Ellie who was fumbling over his shirt buttons.

"Wait Ellie, we have time. I want it to be perfect for you. I want you to have this memory in your soul. Trust me: when you are covered in dust and sand you will need a postcard memory to bring you back home," Rob said.

Ellie felt a bit embarrassed as if he was scolding her; she began to get upset and now her emotions were scattered.  All her self-doubt was creeping back up again and she thought about just walking back to the car and saying, "Fuck you Rob."

Rob looked at her as if he could read her mind, and said, "Darling, don't hear what I'm not saying! I want you like I've never wanted anything before in my life. I just need you to be patient with me. I promise you, I will never hurt you. I need you to trust me. Please?"

Ellie felt a bit better as she watched Rob pitch a tent and lay a blanket for them to sit on. He then called her over with a quick wave. Ellie took two steps forward and once again she was in Rob's warm and secure arms. As Rob softly kissed Ellie's neck he said, " I swear no matter where you are, I promise I will love you and take care of you. Ellie Francis Walker you have tamed my soul and I am yours till the end of time. I will love all your fears, demons, and insecurities away."

Ellie took a deep breath and her mind began to drift back to her current reality. She loved Rob and she was happy they were together; however, today she had to focus on her mission. Ellie closed her eyes one last time to recall the memory of their love-making and gim whispering "Darling, I believe in you. Ellis Francis Walker, I love you for eternity."  Ellie then opened her eyes and told herself she would have a lifetime of sunrises and sunsets with Rob, but today she had to focus on the mission.Her orders were simple: they were to take supplies to the far west side of the region and provide aid to those affected by the bombing in Herat, Afghanistan. There were several thousands of people who were displaced and in need of medical attention. Once the supplies arrived in the area, Ellie's team was to establish a makeshift hospital, provide the aid needed and create a safe "zone." Moreover, in an area like Herat, E. F. Walker's leadership would be tested and it was critical to prove that women were not second-class citizens.

Ellie took one last look in the mirror and made sure her uniform was all in order. "I am a Marine," she told herself. For a few seconds her thoughts went back home to those calm and relaxing days she spent at the ranch with her brother Billie, and his girl, Sabina. Ellie closed her eyes and allowed her thoughts to take her home to a more familiar place. She remembers the last time they were all together. Billie was like a brother; he took care of her after her real brother, Scott, had died fighting in the same war. She remembers his wife, Sabina, a strong courageous Deputy Sheriff who took her in like a sister. Then there was Billie's dad, Ben, who always loved and treated her like a daughter. That was something Ellie desperately needed after her parents had passed away and Scott was killed in action.

Ellie could not help but think of the love of her life: Rob. Commander Robert Stevens, U.S. Army and the man of her dreams. She had been through the ringer and back when it came to relationships. Relationships, what a joke? Ellie laughed because she really had only one before she found Rob. But that one was enough to last her a miserable lifetime. Rob came into her life right when Ellie needed a compass. She was so happy to have Rob in her life, he was her true North. Military life was in her blood and Officer Training School was not easy. Rob made all the madness make sense. She could not imagine her life without him.

Ellie's memories traveled to her time during basic training which was a particularly hard time and when she felt particularly vulnerable. Military life was all Ellie wanted for herself. Her focus was to be the best and that meant becoming a United States Marine. Her brother Scott never approved of her joining the Marines. He knew she had the stamina for the job, but he thought most Marines were arrogant. Ellie wanted to prove Scott wrong and thus used all her time and energy preparing to be the best that she could be. This left no time during her high school for dating, hanging out or making friends. As she entered the Core, Ellie found herself a bit shiny and naïve to the rest of the world.

She fell hard for Axel Cord, a California darling with big plans for his future. His father had secured him a commission even though he did not make the cut. He was set for the Naval Academy but needed to make it through basic training first. Axel immediately took to Ellie, who was willing to help him get through each task. Ellie was always willing to help and make the best of everything. She did not mind the hard work, Axel on the other hand hated everything. He complained about every run, every training mission, the food, the accommodations, and his life overall. Axel was bitter and angry; he hated military life, but his father wanted him to be an Officer. In order to secure himself a future with his father's wealth, he joined up.

Ellie had an uncanny ability to make friends fast and had the type of personality where no one was a stranger. In other words, she was kind to all who were around her and felt the need to help her friends in basic training which demonstrated the leader she was. It was an amazing time for Ellie to grow and establish herself in her career. She was first in every event, every class, and every skill. Ellie was very well-liked and respected by her peers and her leadership team for her confidence and professionalism. Soon Ellie was selected to be team leader which made everyone happy. Well everyone but Axel who would not, could not get over the fact that Ellie had beaten him in every event.

Axel and Ellie started dating while they were in basic training. They would hang out together through the grueling exercises. She was much faster than he was, but no matter what, Ellie would wait for Axel. He proclaimed that he was the best, but everyone knew the truth. Axel boasted about his strength and tight body. He had no workout ethic and his lack of commitment was seen by all. Axel looked good, with his bulging muscles and tan skin but that was all. He never made the effort to make himself or anyone else be better. Axel was just picture perfect, but a fake through and through.

While Ellie's career was emerging as a leader, Axel's took a dive. Ellie was going places and all Axel could do was hang on to her so he would not be left behind. Axel would try to break Ellie's strive by pointing out her flaws and mistakes. And it did not take long for Axel to be knocking her down for every little thing she did or did not do. Ellie tried hard not to let Axel get into her head, but on most days he prevailed.

Ellie was not worried about Axel and his nonsense. She would excuse him by saying stuff like, "that is just Axel being Axel," or "Axel has a lot of his father's personality in him. "It is just Ace, you know he is an Ace." Axel liked being called Ace, however, his peers added "Hole" making him "Acehole." Ellie would never call him Acehole, she would go about her business and forget every mean and rude thing Axel would say. Ellie only focused on the good things and dismissed the bad. Axel however, grew bitter as the days moved forward. He found himself in Ellie's shadow and he could simply not handle it.

One day Axel found himself devastated because once again Ellie had beaten him during morning calisthenics. He was sick and tired of everything Ellie. His group of buddies were giving him a hard time about how a 'chick' had taken him down during defensive tactics. Axel tried to tell them he let her win, but they didn't believe him. Axel was getting angrier and was out for blood. He went to find Ellie because she was the cause of all his misfortune and he was going to get his pound of flesh.

Axel found Ellie alone in the barracks. She was getting ready for an evening to blow some steam with her girlfriends. "What the fuck Ellie! You embarrassed me with the guys! You know I am not allowed to use all my strength during training. You cheated! You know you cheated. Why did you not come clean?"

"No way Axel. I got you good and it was straight. I am not sure why you are complaining about you getting second place," Ellie said, "Or first loser" Ellie taunted.

Axel started seeing red and he pushed Ellie against the wall. He started to choke her with an arm bar to her neck, "get out of that, number one."

Ellie was struggling to catch her breath and she tried to push Axel off of her. "Come on number one, do something" he said.

Ellie kicked at him and connected with his knee which forced him to take a step back and release his grasp on her. Ellie caught her breath as she asked, "What the hell Axel? Why are you so upset? I was just kidding with you."

Axel responded by giving her one quick slap across her face causing her lip to bleed.

"You don't have the right to laugh at me. I take crap from everyone else. I will not take that shit from you. You understand?" he said as he took one step closer to her.

Ellie was frightened by his response and she did not really know what to do.

Axel looked at her face and the fear he brought out of her and said, "Oh I am sorry. Ellie I am so sorry. You know how I get. You know the pressure I am under. I am so sorry. I didn't mean to hurt you. Forgive me. Please forgive me. You just got me and you made me do it."

Axel then grabbed Ellie by her shoulders and yelled, "You know I did not mean it right? Now, go get ready and I will see you at the bar later."

Ellie was in shock and she did not know what to do. She cleaned herself up and decided to forget what just happened. It was just Axel being Axel and he promised he would not hurt her again. She just knew not to make fun of him again because Axel was sensitive about it. He was under a lot of pressure from his father, and the guys. She needed to cut him a break, and she needed to relax.

As time moved forward and the couple kept dating, those episodes with Axel were more frequent than Ellie wanted to admit. Axel would be mad or furious about something or other. He would come looking for Ellie and take out his fury on her body. She would take a mouth full of insults or a beating from Axel. He had a hair trigger temper and anything would cause him to blow his top. Ellie started missing training because Axel bruised her ribs or punched her in the back. Axel could not control himself, and Ellie simply could not win these battles.

Ellie finally called home and contacted her brother Scott, who told her to report Axel. He told his baby sister, "Ellie you know I love you with all my heart. You did nothing wrong, but either you report him or I will kill him with my bare hands." It took all the inner strength that Ellie had to make her report to Naval Intelligence and the Military Police. She swore off a complaint against Axel, which was not taken lightly. It was only a matter of a few hours when Axel found himself behind bars and facing a Court Marshall.

Scott and Billie traveled to base to check on Ellie. She knew it was the right thing to do to report Axel, but she still was embarrassed by the situation. Scott advised Ellie to transfer to another base and to sign up for domestic violence counseling. Scott promised Ellie that although Billie and he had come to kick Axel's ass, they were just going to make sure he would be bounced out of the military. Billie and Scott kept their word and Axel was given a DD: Dishonorable Discharge from the Marines and sent out packing to the hills of California.

Ellie shook her head and came back to her present. She was not sure why her mind had taken her down bad memory lane. "That was years ago with Axel and me. God, what is the matter with me? I need to pull myself together. Okay First Lt. Walker, get your mind straight and get your shit together." She could not shake that bad feeling in the pit of her stomach, but the mission would not wait for her. Ellie took the picture of her parents in her hand and gave it a big kiss. She then grabbed her Saint Christopher medal and placed it in her front top pocket. "Ready, set, go," she said to herself.